THE HAUNTED HOUSE.

BOOK TWO — BENJAMIN LANE

The Haunted House

Book Two — BENJAMIN LANE

By
Joan Williams

Omni Publishers
Post Office Box 603 Escondido, CA 92025

2nd Printing - 1978

Library of Congress Cataloging in Publication Data

Williams, Joan, Date-
The haunted house.

CONTENTS: book 1. Percy.--book 2 Benjamin Lane.
I. Title.
PZ4.W72618Hau [PS3573.I44938] 813'.5'4
ISBN 0-89127-002-7 (v. 1) 78-19149
ISBN 0-89127-005-1 (v. 2)

Printed and Published in the United States

To my loving husband, BILL

Thelma's particular gifts of Extra Sensory Perception are chronicled in Book Two as they continue unfolding throughout her high school years. The intuitional flashes, previsions, and so on, narrated in Book One, are now enhanced by her own attempts at evaluating them as they occur ever involving higher planes of her consciousness.

In Book Two Thelma is being prepared, it seems, to cope with an adulthood of existing in both worlds of consciousness at the same time, as is depicted in Book Three.

Although all the characters in this book are fictitious, and any resemblance to actual persons, living or dead, is purely coincidental, nevertheless, all the psychic phenomena described are based on actual experiences as observed by the author.

Chapter 1

What a difference between Johnnie's high school graduation day and his college graduation today, I was saying to myself as I set the table for lunch and helped Aunt Cora bring in the food.

Johnnie was up in his room rehearsing his speech and waiting to be called for lunch. Uncle Eric was at the university already. He went in the morning and said he would meet us later when we came for the Commencement exercises.

I was not going to say anything about this day being so different, but I knew inside of me that Aunt Cora was remembering, too. She was very quiet all morning and only being extra busy and fussy about Uncle Eric's not forgetting to have some lunch, and Johnnie being sure to get a haircut and me getting dressed up in time to go to the graduation and not keep everybody waiting. Seeing as Johnnie got a haircut yesterday, and I was almost always the first one to be ready and waiting downstairs, her fussiness showed that she was thinking hard about something else.

But, it was Johnnie himself who started talking about what Aunt Cora and I were thinking, as we sat at the table and ate.

"I want you to know, Aunt Cora," he began, "that I owe a whale of a lot to you."

"Oh, go on—," she started to say and he interrupted her.

"No, you have to hear me out, Aunt Cora. Four years ago, on my high school graduation day, things looked so bleak that I thought nothing in the world could make my life any better. You cannot imagine my total misery."

He was still for a bit and we did not say anything. I looked at Aunt Cora and her eyes were all filled with tears.

And then Johnnie went on, "In a way, my dear Aunt, you were an inspiration to me. You gave me courage and the will to go on by your example."

"Me?" Aunt Cora's eyes opened wide and she put down her cup.

"Yes, you! On the day of my high school graduation, you stopped feeling sorry for yourself and set about making your own dream come true as well as taking care of Bunnie and me. You did not have to do it. You had no obligation toward us. But, you worked at getting this house, and you married the professor, and you educated yourself, and you are still working hard in making a wonderful life for all of us. I just want you to know how much it all means to me and how grateful I am for all of it. I would not be getting my degree today if it were not for you. Frankly, I would have had to give up the scholarship and go find work somewhere after high school. But, you made me go on even after I gave up."

Johnnie got up and went over to Aunt Cora. He put his arms around her and kissed her cheek. She hugged him as he knelt at her side, and wiped her eyes as he got up.

"Don't kid yourself, Johnnie lad," she said. "I was scared stiff myself. There's many a day I wondered how we would make it tomorrow. Life's funny, though. Just when you think you have reached the limit, you come to the only course of action you can take—if you're not too scared to do it—and it takes you over the top.

"Come on, now—," she pushed Johnnie a little. "Go finish your lunch and let's get going. We are supposed to be at the university in a couple of hours and there's still a lot to do."

I almost started to cry when Johnnie was talking because my heart got so filled with love.

I used to read in love stories, which I had discovered only a short while ago, how wonderfully happy it is to be in love. Well, it was not true. I was madly in love and completely miserable at the same time.

Of course nobody knew that I was in love with Stephen. And I would not let anybody know about it, either. It was my very own deep dark secret, and it made me so sick inside. The worst thing was that he was graduating from high school himself, and I was only a junior. I had to be going another year and would not even get to see him at school. Not even once a day. Right now, I did not know how I could live through it.

Well, at least now I knew how poor Clifford had felt about me such ages ago when I graduated from grammar school and he walked me home. At least he got to hold my hand and almost kissed me if Percy had not shown up.

And that got me to thinking about Percy. But, before I could get deep into remembering about Percy, the doorbell rang and Aunt Cora asked me to see who it was. I was finished anyway and had excused myself to go when Aunt Cora asked me to see who was at the door.

I almost fell over when I opened the door because there was Stephen, and he was looking so nervous. My own hands were shaking and I could not say anything because I could not breathe with my throat feeling so tight. I could see that Stephen kept swallowing and trying to say something.

Finally, he said in a small voice, "I—I want to tell you something —er, Thelma. No! I mean I want to ask you something!"

I took a deep breath and said, "Oh, sure— Come in," and held the door wide.

He came in slowly and I saw him look all around at all of Aunt Cora's and the professor's beautiful things, and the carvings and mirrors and paintings and things that he could see from the hallway. So I shut the door and went ahead of him into the library, while I waved to him to follow me.

"Like to sit down?" I pointed to one of the chairs.

"No— I— er, I better stand— "

Just then Aunt Cora came into the doorway, and I said to her, "Um, this is Stephen Seliski— somebody I know from school, Aunt Cora. Er— this is my aunt, Mrs. Hawkins," I said to Stephen.

He hesitated a little bit, then went quickly forward and held out his hand. "How do you do. I— I came to ask Thelma to go to the Senior Prom with me tonight."

"Oh! Oh— er— I see. Excuse me. Nice to have met you," and she backed away. I heard her say to herself, "Tonight?"

"Gee, whilikers!" Stephen hit his forehead with his hand. "I did it all wrong. I better go home."

"No! Wait!" I ran after him and stood with my back to the front door.

"I came to ask you and I had to tell it to your aunt first. That was dumb." He looked miserable.

I was so excited. Me, a junior! Going to the Senior Prom!

"Wait, Stephen!" It was the first time I used his name in talking to him and it sounded so sweet and wonderful. "Let me ask my aunt. If she says 'All right', I'll go with you. You want to wait until I find out?"

"I guesso."

I left him standing in the hallway and ran through the dining room into the kitchen. Johnnie was helping Aunt Cora, but when I came in, they both stopped to look at me.

"May I go to the Senior Prom, Aunt Cora?" I asked her.

"Do you want to?"

I nodded.

"At such short notice?"

"He probably got stood up," Johnnie commented.

"I don't care! I'm just a junior, and I got asked to go to the Senior Prom! Can you imagine? Well, gee whiz! Maybe I'm the only junior that got asked!"

Aunt Cora turned to Johnnie. "Do you think it's all right?"

He shrugged. "If she wants to go, I don't see any harm in it."

I ran over to hug him.

"Well, I suppose it's all right," Aunt Cora said to me. So I hugged her, too, and ran back to Stephen.

"I'd love to go to the Senior Prom with you," I said to him.

"You would?!"

I nodded and we both started to laugh.

"What time?" I finally asked.

"Eight o'clock. O.K.?"

"Yeah, O.K. Eight o-clock."

"I gotta go now," said Stephen as he opened the door and went.

I was so happy, and the hurt went away from my heart at being so madly in love. I just sat on the stairs and smiled a mysterious smile.

"What are you mooning about?" Johnnie was asking me. I had not even seen him coming.

"I'm going to the Senior Prom," I said dreamily.

Johnnie squatted down to stare into my face. "Ain't that the cat's pajamas!" he said in a marvelling voice.

I pushed him till he fell over, but he grabbed my ankle and I got pulled off the step onto the floor near him. Johnnie sat up and put his face close to mine. "How long have you known this guy?"

"All of last year. I first noticed him in my morning study period when his seat was next to mine. And then we used to wave to each other in the hall between classes. And we had the same study period in the afternoon. We started talking when he asked to borrow my pencil. And once he asked for some sheets out of my notebook because he had used up all of his.

"And then some afternoons when he did not have football practice, he walked home with me as far as the avenue. He lives on Benjamin Lane and our back fence is on Benjamin Lane."

By this time Johnnie was sitting cross-legged in front of me. He said, "You mean to tell me that you've been carrying on with some gazook, and we didn't even know about it?"

I jumped up and I was indignant. "What do you mean, Johnnie? Who's carrying on? We just talked about school things. And don't call him a gazook!"

"Sorry. Am I hearing right? You've known this ga — er — guy all of last year and you never mentioned anything about him to us? So why didn't you ask him to go to your Junior Prom?"

"Because he's a senior, don't you understand?"

"No."

"Honestly, Johnnie! For somebody so smart to get a university scholarship at Brown and graduating with honors and getting a degree and all, you can be so dumb."

Johnnie rolled his eyes up. "Women!" Then he squinted his eyes and asked, "Has it occurred to you, young lady, that he may have been turned down a few times since he asks you on the very day of the prom?"

"Oh, you're just too smart! And has it occurred to you that Stephen may have been too nervous to ask me before because I could have said, 'No'? But he had to know and he came at the last minute just to make sure and not really expecting me to say, 'Yes', because it was too late. And maybe he wanted to give me a chance to say 'No', because it was too late and that would not make him feel so bad. Is that clear?"

"Not really," and Johnnie scrambled up to his feet. "But give me a little time and it will sort itself out into some semblance of coherence. All of your maybes do not convince me of the reason in back of the guy's asking you to go at the last minute."

I wanted to thump him on the back, but with his long legs he ran up two steps at a time and I could not catch up with him.

As I was dressing to go to Johnnie's graduation, I remembered that I was supposed to help Aunt Cora tonight with some kind of a reception and buffet supper in our dining room and dance in our living room for a bunch of Johnnie's friends from the university. So I went over and knocked on his door. When he opened it, he flung up his arm and peered at me over it.

"Oh, Johnnie! I just remembered! I was supposed to help Aunt Cora with your party tonight!"

"Don't worry about that. Tell you what I will do. I'll help Aunt Cora tonight. O.K.? Now, hurry up and don't keep Aunt Cora waiting while I dash off to get my auto to take us all to the Commencement. And you let me do all the talking when we see Uncle Eric. Right after the exercises, you and I, Aunt Cora and Uncle Eric will leave as soon as possible to get everything set up for the party tonight. And when we get home, you go right upstairs and get yourself dolled up in that pink dress you got for tonight to wear at my party, and go to the prom."

I flung my arms around him and hugged him with all my might. "You are the bestest brother ever and I could love you forever."

He hugged me back, and laughed, "Is that a promise? Gee, how lucky can a guy get?"

Well, nobody was more surprised than I when Uncle Eric was delighted that I was going to the Senior Prom. They were glad because it made up for my not going to my Junior Prom.

I remembered how my best friend, Eda, was bragging every time she came over that she was going to the Junior Prom with the quarterback of our varsity football team. And when Aunt Cora, or Uncle Eric or Johnnie asked me if I were going, I said that I did not feel like asking anybody, and that nobody asked me, and I did not care if I went or not. I guess that they did not believe me.

How could they know that I would not have gone even if anyone else besides Stephen had asked me. I was in love with him and love was awful. I really felt sick. My chest had an ache in it all the time and my breath was short. All I could think of all the time was Stephen and how I wanted to be in the same room with him all day. If only I could touch him. The thought of my kissing him made me feel faint. I could not eat much, I could not sleep good, and all I did was mope around. I really had to force myself to do my homework.

I caught Aunt Cora looking at me in a strange way. And when I caught her, she turned away quickly. I did not want anybody to know how awful I felt because vacation was coming and I did not know if I would be seeing Stephen at all every day like I used to, even if he did live across the back fence from me.

I had a perfect attendance record in my junior year. I went to school every day even though I did not feel like it sometimes. Doing any homework in study hall was impossible because I was always conscious of him. I sat sort of sideways so I could see him even though I held my book up and pretended that I was reading. I noticed that he used to sit sort of sideways, too, and once in awhile I would catch him looking at me, but he would look away real quick.

So, anyway, I guessed that Aunt Cora and Uncle Eric thought I was moping because nobody asked me to go to the Junior Prom, which was all over having been held last week. And maybe Aunt Cora bought me that beautiful pink dress to wear to Johnnie's party so it would make up for my not going to the Junior Prom.

"Thelma, you're a real sneak sometimes," Eda said when she came over to go with us to Johnnie's Commencement even though I did not remember if anybody asked her, and after Aunt Cora told her so casually that we would be hurrying back right after the ceremonies because I had to get ready to go to the Senior Prom at the high school.

"Who are you going with? Why didn't you tell me? We're best

friends and I tell you everything, don't I?"

How could I tell her that I had nothing to tell before today? So I sort of shrugged and said offhanded like, "Oh, Stephen Seliski asked me, but I wasn't sure because of Johnnie's Commencement on the same day and Johnnie's party after that on the same evening and I was supposed to help Aunt Cora with the refreshments and all," I said with a straight face as if it was no big thing in my life to be going to the Senior Prom. And all the while I was talking, I was so excited that it was the happiest day of my life.

Then Eda started begging Aunt Cora to let her help instead of me helping. She said that her grandmother would let her stay and help as long as she wanted. And, besides, she had already told her grandmother that she might spend the night at our house and had brought her pajamas and toothbrush in the paper bag, anyway.

Aunt Cora shot a look at Johnnie, who looked up at the ceiling and tried to keep a straight face. Eda always wanted to be in on everything in our family. She was very pushy but she was so open about it that nobody could get mad at her. Uncle Eric even had a bet going with Aunt Cora that Eda would marry Johnnie some day. Of course, Johnnie avoided Eda as much as possible, but he was not very successful at it. And she was crazy about Johnnie and did not care who knew it. She had even asked him to take her to the Junior Prom but he told her that he just had to study for some finals. They were over a long time ago, so I stared at him and he said that he had some unfinished business that he had to do. And then the quarterback asked her to go so then she was not so heartbroken. Now, she would be having Johnnie all to herself all evening. She got so busy with that idea that she forgot to pester me about Stephen, and I was glad. It left me to myself to get dressed for the prom while Eda was downstairs helping set up the buffet and getting all the things ready for the party.

I really did look beautiful with my blonde hair piled up on top of my head. My pale pink gown with the silver threads in it looked real nice on me. The skirt had yards and yards of stuff in it and it stood out all around — kind of old fashioned but nice. I was going to wear a deep maroon velvet cape over it and was trying it on when I heard a soft knock on the door and Johnnie's voice asking, "Are you decent?"

"Come in!" I called and he stuck his head in and whistled.

"Oh, boy! You're a knockout! Say, does this Stephen fella have an auto to take you to the prom?"

"I don't know."

"Well, I can take you, if you want. And when you're ready to come home, he can call here and I'll go get you."

"Wait up. I'm ready." I grabbed my evening bag and we both went downstairs.

When we got to the vestibule, we saw Uncle Eric come in his old touring car around from the back and stop it in back of Johnnie's roadster. Then he saw us and said, "Thought I might give the kids a ride in case the young man did not have a machine."

Just then there was a loud backfiring and a very noisy banging and rattling coming up our driveway and a large touring Stutz drove up to our front door. Another couple was in the front seat and Stephen jumped out from in back. He was holding a small box in his hand. I introduced him to Uncle Eric and to Johnnie and they all shook hands and he pinned a gardenia on me and I got in back.

Uncle Eric and Johnnie kept him talking casual like, but they found out more about him in five minutes than I did in a whole year. And then he got in and we drove off. But, just before the driver put the car in gear, he reached back and gave something all folded up to Stephen. I caught a glimpse of it and it was a folded up bill of money, but I did not see for how much. Stephen put it in his pocket and turned to look at me. Then, he took my hand and smiled. I was so happy and felt like a queen. Life was wonderful. I did not remember the names of the other two seniors in the front seat, even though I was introduced as I got into the back seat.

When we got to the hall, the couple in front got right out and went in. We could hear the music of the dance band playing. I leaned forward to get out, too, but Stephen said, "Let's get acquainted first. O.K.?"

So I leaned back and looked at him.

"I got to meet your family—your brother and your aunt and uncle. Do you have a mother and father?"

"They are dead. My brother and I live with my aunt and uncle."

"Oh, I see. That's too bad about your parents. Hey! I never asked you before, but your house is supposed to be haunted. Is it?"

"No, it isn't. If it was, it is not any more," and I laughed.

"Well, I'll tell you something about myself. We are not rich like you. In fact we are poor. My father fell off a crane in the foundry where he was working and hurt his back. He can't walk."

"Oh, I'm so sorry!"

Stephen shrugged. "And there's my mother and my older sister, Mary, who works in Cherry & Webb's. I would have had to quit school and go to work, too, but the company put my father on half-pay and promised me a job when I graduate and if they start hiring again."

After talking awhile, we went in. Once the chaperone told him not to hold me so close. I couldn't remember when I was so happy.

He did not kiss me goodnight, but he kissed my hand and this was the very first time that anybody kissed my hand. I felt like a movie queen. And he thanked me for going to the prom with him.

Chapter 2

It was the first time in ages that I could remember being all alone in the house. It felt restful and safe with all the comfortable sounds around me. The big clock in the hall downstairs banged a half-hour and I sort of wondered what time it was.

A while back Aunt Cora had stuck her head in my room and said that she was going shopping, and I had told her that I would be going to the public library. I had changed my mind about returning a book I had started and did not find interesting enough to go on. And this morning I had opened it in the middle to get my mind off Stephen, and that part was so interesting that I went back to the beginning where I left off and went on reading from there. Since the prom I had not heard from Stephen and could not imagine why. So I tried to find something that would take my mind off him.

When I started reading, I heard Olaf Olafsen, our hired hand, start the old Ford to take Aunt Cora shopping. She did not have to push the baby carriage any more when she went shopping after she got married to the professor, who got so rich from his old uncle.

And Johnnie was called back this morning to help out in the public library until they could find somebody else to work during the summer vacation putting away books like Johnnie used to do. Only now he did not have to go to work any more. The professor even gave Johnnie a roadster and put money in the bank for him. It was funny how we used to call Uncle Eric, "the professor". Johnnie and I did it, as well as Aunt Cora, and that was when he was a boarder and before he married Aunt Cora. Now he really felt like an uncle because he loved us all and was so good to us.

I wondered when Uncle Eric would be back from San Francisco

where he went in a big hurry a week after vacation started. He had some business about the shipping company, I supposed, that his uncle had left him.

I started thinking about Stephen again. The book lay on my lap and I just sat on the window seat and looked out into the garden through the branches of the huge old tree next to my window. Birds were hopping around on the branches and a breeze was rustling the leaves through which it passed on its way to make my window curtains wave now and then.

Being alone in the house made me think of Percy who went away on my grammar school graduation night. I missed him now and it made me think of how long he had been in the boarded up haunted house, maybe almost a hundred years. Being alone now in the house was different. The house was lived in and I could feel Aunt Cora and Uncle Eric and Johnnie around me although they were out, so the house was not haunted any more with Percy gone. Once in awhile when I woke up in the morning I would still look toward the window seat, expecting to see Percy waiting for me to wake up. Then I would feel sorry that I got so mad at him and told him to go away. I never really believed that he would go away and never come back. Then I would sigh and get up. Percy's going away was all because of Clifford's walking me home after the social on graduation night and trying to kiss me in the hallway. Percy showed up and scared him away. It made me cry when Percy spoiled my first kiss by a boy and I yelled at him to go away and that I did not want to see him again, never ever. And he said he would leave, but I did not believe him. He said truly, though, because I no longer felt him in or near the house, so I guessed he was really gone. Maybe his mother came to get him like she did once before and he would not go, but this time he must have gone.

Thinking about Percy made me remember the little trunk in the attic in the secret room behind the chimney, so I got up from the window seat and went up to my parent's room in the attic where we moved their bedroom furniture after Aunt Cora bought the boarded up house with the insurance money we got from the accident when Mom and Dad died.

I pushed the panel near the chimney and went into the secret room to get Percy's little trunk and to look at his things. After awhile I went over to the attic window all covered with dust and which was way up under the roof and over the front door of the house. I pulled on a latch at the side of it and it opened into the house instead of out, and the whole room got real bright.

I went down to the kitchen and got some rags and some water with ammonia in it to wash the window, also a broom and a dust pan to clean the room up. Then I closed the panel near the chimney and the room was real bright. I noticed right away that there was another window just like the first one and it was directly opposite. I had never noticed that particular window before. So I got that one washed and pulled it open to wash the outside, too. And I saw way over beyond our back garden, the upper part of a brick building with a flat roof.

In leaving our house, I usually turned left in going to school, to see Eda, to go to the public library or downtown, the movies and everywhere. After turning left again, I would come to another fence next to ours. Still I knew that there was a little street in back of our house and that Stephen lived on it. So I supposed that if I turned right from our front gate, and by turning right again at the corner, I would come to the street where this building was.

As I was looking at it now, I saw a girl come through the door of a box-like structure on top of the roof. She was carrying a big basket which she put down, and started hanging up some clothes on the lines stretched between poles. And then I almost stopped breathing, I saw a boy come out of the door and even so far away, I knew it was Stephen. He started taking the clothes out of the basket and handing them to the girl to hang up. So that was where he lived! But who was the girl?

And then I got so jealous of the girl that I wanted to cry. It was even worse than being in love. I wanted to know what she looked like and remembered my brother's telescope and ran right down to get it. When I got back, there was no one on the roof any more, only the clothes were there waving on the lines. I could see real good as if I were right there when I put the telescope to my eye and turned a gadget on it to make everything clear. I decided to ask Johnnie if he would let me have the telescope to keep when he came home from the public library later on.

As I was closing the windows, I heard the noise of Uncle Eric's old Ford on our driveway and then I heard the door slam way below. I guessed that Aunt Cora had come back. I started putting Percy's things away into the little old trunk, when I heard the voices of Aunt Cora and Uncle Eric coming up the attic stairs. I was surprised that Uncle Eric had come back, and jumped up to go back through the panel. But I stopped and I did not know why I stopped. Anyway, I sat very still on the floor.

Then I heard a very heavy thing drop on the floor on the other side of the panel and Uncle Eric said, "Well, Cora, there does not seem to be anything else in this carton that you had in your closet except plays and typed parts of plays and some reviews of plays given. Do you remember if you threw away anything at all out of this box?"

"No, I did not throw anything away of theirs, 'specially papers of any kind. Johnnie and I saved everything we could find and put it all in this carton. We looked through everything very carefully for an insurance that either one or the other of them could have paid on even if it had lapsed, but there was no other insurance except the one that I paid on for years and with which I bought this house for the children.

"We found their marriage license, and her and his marriage licenses of their previous marriages. And then there was Aggie's divorce papers from Francis Maloney and Paddy's first wife's death certificate. And we found the kids' certificates and that's how we found out that Paddy was not Bunny's father. And from other things, we discovered that Francis Maloney was Vern Framingham, the movie actor."

Then I heard the rocker start creaking as if one or the other was rocking in it. I also heard the bed creak as if one or the other had sat down on it.

"I'm very disturbed about Bunny," I heard Uncle Eric say. "Not only from the standpoint of our not being able to adopt her when her father is living, but also because she has the name Pendleton on her grammar school graduation diploma when it should be Maloney, which is her legal name. Why, I do not even know if Framingham has had his name changed legally from Maloney to Framingham. With her graduating from high school next June, what name is she going to have on her high school diploma? She has to be told Cora, about her not being related to any of us. And I don't know how to do it."

"I don't, either," Aunt Cora said. "I'm really scared to let her know that she is not related to any of us. We all love her so."

"I do, too. She is a dear lovely child and growing into a very beautiful young lady. And so unusually gifted, as well," said Uncle Eric.

I had to stuff the bottom of my dress into my mouth not to cry out loud when I heard them say how much they loved me, because I loved them all very much, too.

"Well," Uncle Eric sighed. "All we can do now is wait until we hear from Framingham's agent. This whole business of my inheritance, and the shipping company my uncle left me — Gad, am I glad that Captain Olafsen knows about running it. I don't know what I'd do without him — and now this about Thelma's father. It has taken me all this time to even find out how to get in touch with the man. Cora, these past three, almost four years would have worn me down to the ground if it had not been for you, my darling. You sustain me and I love you more than I can express."

Then I heard the rocker creak when someone stood up and then the bed creaked as if some one got off it and two pairs of feet came together, and I guessed that they were kissing.

I just closed my eyes and imagined how it would be if Stephen and I kissed.

After awhile, I heard Uncle Eric say, "Cora, I am not a violent man, but if there was ever a time I wanted to strike a man, it was when that agent of Framingham's tilted back in his chair at the Los Angeles office and said that Framingham had at least two paternity suits a year to deal with. He did not believe me, dear, even after I showed him the birth certificate with Framingham's real name, Francis Maloney, on it. He did tilt forward to study it and then said that the name of Francis Maloney was quite common."

"You mean that Bunny's father is being sued all the time for making babies?" Aunt Cora sounded very shocked.

"It seems so. But the agent, however, hastened to tell me that none of the women ever succeeded in making their allegations stick."

"The nerve of him to talk to you like that!"

"As I said before, Cora, I had no choice but to go to the agent. The studio people insisted that the agent handled all affairs, personal and business, of his client, 'specially when the client was not available in person. And when they told me that Framingham was away on location making a moving picture, I had no other choice but to go to his agent whose name and address the studio gave me."

"Was there anyone in the studio that knew where he lives?"

"He is not with the major studios any more. It seems that his popularity slipped quite a bit when the talkies came in. But he still has a big name so a smaller studio is trying to build his popularity up again. They are gambling on him, I suppose. His being a long-lost father is the last thing they want to cope with."

I got excited about Uncle Eric's actually going to the moving picture studio and wished I could have gone with him. But nobody knew that I knew already about Vern Framingham's being my real father. I was not upset at all. Once in awhile I would think real hard how to let them know that I knew about my real father, without upsetting them. Here they did not want to upset me and I did not want to upset them. But, I could never think of a way to let them know.

Then, I heard Aunt Cora say, "We better go downstairs. Bunny will be coming home pretty soon. She said she was going to the library. Maybe she will come home with Johnnie. And I had better get some dinner started."

I heard them go out, close the door, and go downstairs. They kept on talking and I could tell that they went all the way down to the kitchen. It got real quiet and I did not dare drag Percy's trunk across the floor because it would make a noise so I left it where it was. Then, I pulled the panel back and stepped into the attic room. I saw a big carton in the middle of the floor and wanted to look inside but knew that I had to get downstairs and outside if I did not want Aunt Cora and Uncle Eric to feel badly about my hearing them talk about my real father. So I went real quiet down to the second floor and heard them talking in the kitchen.

The hall was empty and I ran down the stairs and out the side door. I didn't take a deep breath until I was in the gazebo. There were a lot of trees and bushes between the gazebo and the house. Captain Olafsen had fixed the fountain and made the water pump from the well work and the fountain was going. There were statues around, so if anybody was in the gazebo, nobody could see them from the house, or from the stable, carriage house, or shed. It was a small park in this part of our front yard.

Then I looked back toward the back of our grounds, and jumped up to go clear to the farthest end in order to see if the building I saw from the attic was next to our back fence. The path farthest from our house went past the stable, then past a small greenhouse, then through our orchard, and there was the iron fence that Captain Olafsen had painted. I was so disappointed that all along the back fence, the bushes had never been taken out, but through some of the growth I could see that there still was the tall wooden old fence that used to be all around the other sides of the house when we first moved in. Over to the side of our fence I could see the very top of the house and it seemed to be on the other side of the street.

So I went back the way I came and went in through the kitchen door.

"There you are," said Aunt Cora. "Wash your hands, Honey, and set the table, will you?"

So I washed my hands at the kitchen sink and Aunt Cora said, "Uncle Eric is back from California and he helped me carry up a box of plays and all kinds of magazines and things that belonged to your Ma up to the attic."

"Oh?" I tried to sound surprised. "After I set the table, may I run up and look at them, Aunt Cora? May I?"

"Sure. I'll call you when dinner is ready."

The table got set awfully quick and I was back in the attic room and opening the cardboard box before Aunt Cora could change her mind.

Most of the things on top were plays and I saw Mom's writing and lines drawn under some of the sentences. I could even smell her perfume and felt her as if she had been around just before and went off to the theater for awhile but would be back soon. I did not feel sad at all.

As I picked up each thing, I went through it page by page to see what she had written in the margins. Things like "walk away and turn after two steps" or "snap fingers" or "pick up cigarette" and things like that. Some of the plays had markers in them like a hairpin or a gum wrapper or a match where she had left off reading.

Then I heard Aunt Cora calling and went downstairs. I knew where I would be spending the next week maybe, or however long it would take me to go through all the stuff in the box.

Of course, I had not let anybody know that I had a bunch of magazines under my window seat in my room and they all had something about Vern Framingham in them. Some of the magazines I got from Eda, and some I bought with my allowance. There were lots of pictures of my father with different actresses at parties and premieres and he looked so handsome in the different kinds of clothes he was wearing, but best of all in a tuxedo. The magazines were always saying that he was with Myra Allan and in the pictures she looked a little bit like Mom but not much because Mom was more beautiful.

Chapter 3

In the next few days, I kept thinking how I could get to see Stephen again. Maybe I could go over to Benjamin Lane as if I were only taking a walk. Every time I remembered how he had held my hand and put his arm around me when we were dancing, I would feel all soft and swoony. I could not imagine why he never came back. Was it something I did or said?

And thinking of how I felt about Stephen, made me remember how Clifford Peters used to look at me and how he walked me home after my grammar school graduation and how he wanted to kiss me.

While thinking about Clifford Peters and how he was the first boy who tried to kiss me, it made me recall a dream I had about him once. After waking up, I lay a long time thinking about the dream and wondering if I should tell it to Aunt Cora and see what she thought of it.

In my dream I was walking along a very wide street and it was very sunny and warm on my side. I heard somebody call my name from the other side and I looked across the street and saw Clifford. He called for me to go over to his side but I said for him to come over to my side because it was sunny and warm while his side was in the shade. But he said he could not cross the street, so I went over and it was very cold. He took my hand and we ran and ran until we came to a big gate standing open and it was so beautiful inside the gate. The flowers were so beautiful and the colors so bright, and there were birds singing like a hundred canaries going all at once! It was even more beautiful than our garden at home that Mr. Olafsen kept looking so nice all the time.

When we came to the gate, Clifford said that he had to go in and wanted me to go with him, but something made me stop and I took my hand away from his. I asked him that if I went in, could I come out again because there was a very nice man standing at the gate who was waiting for Clifford to go in and then he would close the gate. So Clifford asked the man if I could get out again should I go inside and the man smiled and said that the gate could be opened only once in a long while. If I went inside, I would have to wait a long time before I could get out again.

So I said to Clifford, "I can't go with you, Clifford. My aunt and uncle and my brother would not like it at all. I have to go back."

"Well, I'll wait for you when you can come, all right?" he asked.

He walked backwards until he was inside and the man closed the gate. I started walking near the fence and Clifford walked along the fence, too, on the inside and we talked about things. Then I came to the place where I had crossed the street and said, "So long, Clifford, I have to go now," and ran across to the sunny side where it was nice and warm. When I got across, I turned and waved to him and he waved back.

I heard him call, "I'll be waiting for you, Thelma!"

He looked so sad and alone and I felt sorry that I could not keep him company, but had to go home because everybody was waiting for me. After that I woke up, then I remembered that I lay awake and thought of the dream for a long time.

It must be the middle of the morning I decided, and here I have been lying in bed thinking first about Stephen and then about poor Clifford. I sighed and got out of bed. How nice summer vacations are, I decided, when I could get up any time I wanted to. And I could do my chores any time I wanted to, as long as I did them each day.

Aunt Cora was surprised when I came down to the kitchen because it was so early and I had thought all the time that it was real late. I told her that I would do my chores right away after breakfast because I wanted to go up to the attic and look at all the things in the big box that Uncle Eric had taken up there.

"There's a small bookcase out in the carriage house, Bunny, that is maybe just big enough to hold all those papers and notebooks and plays put on the shelves," Aunt Cora said. "If you want it, I could help you take it up to the attic when you are ready."

I hurried upstairs to make the beds, dust all around, tidy up the bathrooms and came back to the kitchen so Aunt Cora could get the bookcase, but Mr. Olafsen was already coming in the back door, carrying the bookcase in one hand. Aunt Cora suggested he take it right upstairs to the attic, and I eagerly followed close behind him.

The bookcase was a wonderful idea because I could separate the plays from the books and other things and put them on separate shelves. As I took each thing up, I went through all the pages to see what Mom or Dad wrote and I found all kinds of other things besides books and plays. There was even a cigar box with a lipstick in it, some matches, a pair of earrings, and a wedding ring. So, any time that I found anything different, like a valentine or a letter, I put it into the cigar box. Some of the cards and letters were stuck so hard between the pages that I had to pull real hard to get them apart. I guessed they had been there a long time and the books had not been opened in a long time.

Every time I found a letter, I looked inside for other things besides writing and found a lot of pictures like that. I guessed some of them were of me because Mom was holding a baby and it looked something like me. I even found the scrapbook of Vern Framingham that I had heard Aunt Cora tell Uncle Eric about on their wedding night. I guessed that Aunt Cora forgot to remove it.

It was when I picked up a play that I saw it was two plays stuck together when I started looking through the first one, page by page. I saw that each had been mended and the paste had run out along the side of one which made it stick to the other one. There was a plain envelope between the plays and one side of it was stuck to the back of one of them. If you looked real quick, you could not see the envelope, but I was going page by page, looking for writing, and so I found it.

I pulled the envelope out real careful so as not to tear the cover off the play and looked inside. It was not a letter but there was some sort of paper inside, which I unfolded and started to look at.

It was about me. It said how I was adopted by Patrick Pendleton and that my name was changed from Thelma Maloney to Thelma Pendleton. I didn't know what to do, so I just sat and thought and looked at the paper for a long time. It came to me that my father must have given his permission to have my name changed. It made my heart ache real hard that he cared so little about me. Then I got up from the floor and went down to my room and sat on the window seat and thought some more and looked at the paper some more.

After a long while, I heard Uncle Eric's old Ford come through our front gate and drive around the house to the stable. Then, I heard Uncle Eric's and Johnnie's voices downstairs and guessed that Uncle Eric had stopped by the library and brought Johnnie home for lunch. The hum of voices got louder and I heard Johnnie run up the stairs and call me as he turned at the top of the stairs and started up the attic stairs.

I got up and walked toward the door. I reached it as Johnnie came running down from the attic. He stopped when he saw me.

"Lunch is ready," he said. He just stared at me and I stared back. "Anything the matter?" he asked.

When I did not answer, he came over and shook my arm a little. The paper fell to the floor. He picked it up and looked at it.

"Oh, God!" he said. "Where did you get this?"

"I found it in the box upstairs."

"When?"

"A little while ago."

He drew a big breath and put his arm around my shoulders. Then he said, "Well, I guess the time has come. Let's go downstairs."

So we went together to the dining room just as Aunt Cora came in carrying a platter full of toasted cheese sandwiches and a pot of coffee. Uncle Eric, carrying a soup tureen, followed her.

They both stopped suddenly when they saw Johnnie and me just like Johnnie had stopped when he saw me at the door of my room.

"What's the matter?" Aunt Cora asked.

Johnnie walked over to her and gave her the adoption paper after she put down the platter and coffee pot.

"Bunny found this in the box upstairs," he said.

Uncle Eric put down the tureen and bent over to look at the paper, too.

Nobody said anything for a long while. We just stood and looked at each other after Aunt Cora and Uncle Eric finished looking at the paper. Uncle Eric was the first to move and he came to me awfully quick and put both his hands on my shoulders.

"This is the best and greatest thing that could have happened to us. Your aunt and I have been coping with the problem related to this paper ever since the trouble that came up with your transfer to the Spring Street School."

He led me to my seat at the table and we all sat down. Then Aunt Cora started to cry, so I got up again and went over to her to put my arms around her and hug her.

Uncle Eric went on talking. "Your aunt found all the documents pertaining to the family and these indicated that your mother had been married before and you had been born prior to her marriage to Johnnie's father shortly after her divorce from your father. Do you understand what I am saying, Bunny?" He looked very anxious.

I nodded and he went on. "In order to institute adoption proceedings, your aunt had to produce your birth certificate among other things, and when she saw that the name differed on your birth certificate, she was very much surprised, since she had not known about your mother's previous marriage. Johnnie had been with his maternal grandparents when his own mother died and then was in an orphanage for a short while when his grandfather died, and his grandmother could not take care of him. Then his father and his second wife—your mother, Bunny—brought him home to live with them. Johnnie assumed that you were his half-sister, and that his father was your father. The fact of the matter is, that you are not related to anyone here at all. That is, blood related, you understand. However, this paper brings you into the family legally. Let me hasten to add, Bunny, that you are most dear to all of us and we love you as much, and perhaps more, than many parents care for their own children. You know this, don't you, dear?"

I nodded again because my throat was too full to talk. Aunt Cora started filling everyone's plates, so I went to my seat and sat down.

Uncle Eric went on. "Your aunt and Johnnie learned the true relationship when they went through the box that I carried up to the attic. They gathered all the papers and locked them up for safekeeping. And when the problem of your custody came up at your transfer to Spring Street School, your aunt's marriage to me served to delay the problem, although it still existed in our minds.

"Also, we know the identity of your father. He happens to be Vern Framingham, the moving picture actor."

All through Uncle Eric's explanations I tried not to show that I already knew everything he was telling me because I had heard Aunt Cora tell him practically all of it on their wedding night. So I just kept looking at him and nodding once in awhile. I even opened my eyes wide when he said that Vern Framingham was my father as if I did not have a bunch of movie stories about my father, which I kept under my window seat.

Everyone was eating now, but Uncle Eric was still talking between mouthfuls.

"All through the period following your aunt's and my marriage when I was involved with the business of my inheritance, every spare moment I could get, I kept going to the problem of adopting you. In my consultations with an attorney, I was advised what documents were needed in order to institute proceedings. It was necessary to arrange a meeting with your father to acquaint him with your aunt's and my desire to adopt you. Unfortunately, I have not been able to contact your father and had to leave my written request with his agent as well as a copy of your birth certificate.

"All through this, our biggest worry was how to let you know that all this activity was going on, which concerns you most vitally. How to let you know that you have a father and a famous one, at that. We did not want to cause you a state of shock. Do you understand our concern?"

"I think so," I said in a small voice. How could I let them know at this time that I knew already about Vern Framingham being my father? I didn't know what to do. I loved them all as much as they loved me.

I pushed my chair back and asked to be excused. I had to go outside and sit in the gazebo and think, while the fountain splashed and the birds made chirping noises.

For some reason, all I could think of, was Clifford for quite awhile, as I sat in the gazebo.

I remembered that summer after I graduated from grammar school, and how it went by like a wink. Part of its going by so fast was that Eda and her grandmother asked me to stay at their cottage on Rocky Point the whole summer. Their family was extra special nice, now that Mr. Olafsen—I should have said Captain Olafsen—was working for Uncle Eric and running one of his ships.

Eda did not want to live in San Francisco. She told me how she cried and carried on to go back to stay with her grandmother in Providence. And her grandmother would not go to live with Eda's mother and Captain Olafsen, either, because she was mad at him for staying away such a long time when he had promised to marry Eda's mother way back when they lived in Italy.

So Eda came back to stay with her grandmother and Captain Olafsen sent money to them every week. It was really Uncle Eric who got a bank in San Francisco to send a check to Eda's grandmother because the captain asked him to. Eda said that her mother did not mind her going back to Providence because she made a lot of friends in the Italian section of San Francisco which was every bit as big as the one in Providence.

Meanwhile, all during the summer that I was at Eda's on Rocky Point, Johnnie and Captain Olafsen's son, who was now our hired hand, took the captain's plans for fixing up the carriage house, and did the whole job for Johnnie.

Aunt Cora helped Johnnie in getting the place furnished after it was painted, and Johnnie moved all his things in. He had made some new friends at Brown and all his old friends from high school got to visiting him and he liked having his very own place.

Anyway, all the time I was at Rocky Point, Johnnie came every Saturday in his roadster and brought all kinds of things to eat which lasted practically all week. After awhile Eda's grandmother got to giving him a list of what to bring the following week. I guessed it was Aunt Cora's way of paying the grandmother for having me at their place. And Johnnie sometimes stayed over a day or so if he felt like it. It was comical to watch Eda's grandmother and Johnnie talking to each other, because she could speak practically no English and he could speak no Italian and they wound up yelling at each other until Eda came to explain things. But the grandmother cooked real fancy dishes when Johnnie came and was so pleased when he showed her how much he liked everything.

And then Eda got a wild crush on Johnnie. She moped all week and watched the street all Saturday until she saw his roadster and then she would start to act as if she didn't care that he came. She was so good at it that Johnnie never guessed she was so wild about him. I never said anything to anybody about it. So Johnnie would swim with Eda and me, play ball on the beach with us and take us on the rides in the amusement park, sometimes.

In no time at all, it seemed, it was the first day of high school and Eda came over to go to school with me. She was so excited. At last she was going to be in the same school again with me.

I will never forget that first day in high school. I had a funny feeling inside of me that the next four years would not be any fun at all, and I also got a very sad feeling as if something awful would happen.

When we got to the high school, we saw signs saying that all freshmen had to go to the auditorium and sit alphabetically by our last names. So that's when I saw Clifford again. We both went to the same section under "P" because he was Peters and I was Pendleton. Eda went to the "O" section because she was Olafsen now since her mother married the captain and she was not Pelucca any more.

We got called up front and programs were given to us. Clifford and I had the same programs and the same Home Room, but Eda's was all different. The only same periods she had with me were lunch and gym.

It was all so different because we had to change rooms for different periods and I did not like it at all. I felt I was not me any more, just one of a great big bunch of people. I felt as if I was all alone in a canoe or something and had to paddle around all by myself as best I could, and everybody was too busy to care much about me. And I was sorry that I would not have much chance to get to know any of my teachers real good. They all had so many pupils that I was just a name to them, and I wondered if they would ever connect my name with my face. I wished I was back at good old Spring Street Grammar School again.

I even had two men teachers, and one of them asked me if I was related to John Pendleton. That was my history teacher who made us sit alphabetically and when he called my name, he stopped and looked at me over his glasses, and asked me.

"He is my brother," I said as I went to my seat.

Everybody turned around to look at me. The teacher did not say anything else but went on calling other names.

After school, Clifford walked home with Eda and me and he looked so white and tired. When we came to the avenue, Eda went on to her house and Clifford walked with me to our front gate. When I turned to say "So long," to him, a funny thing happened. His face sort of faded out and all I saw were his two eyes, and the blue of them burned like the blue part of a gas flame. I blinked and his face appeared again, and then I felt as if a hand closed over my heart and squeezed it. I did not like the feeling at all. I never forgot the experience.

And all through my freshman year, Clifford used to walk part way home with Eda and me, and we used to talk about all kinds of things but mostly about school.

Since his name and mine began with the same letter, we always sat not far from each other in all the classes where we were seated alphabetically. Sometimes we helped each other. Anyway, Clifford was so smart and not because he studied. I had to work very hard to get A's and B's, but all he had to do was look at things once and he knew right away what it was all about. He could do arithmetic in his head faster than we all could do it on paper.

He was small like me and so pale. He had no color in his face at all. Sometimes as he talked, I would get so sad and would not know why. But his eyes always shone more brightly than anyone else's. I had never seen brighter ones.

And when fall was over and winter came, it got to be very cold some days and Clifford would shiver and his teeth would chatter so he could hardly talk and we would run to keep warm. And even when we got out of breath, we would walk fast, and hold hands. I loved talking with him because he was more than smart. I bet he was a genius.

Then he did not come to school for a long time. And one day our Home Room teacher told us that Clifford was sick and had gone to a sanatorium. And that was all I heard of him the rest of the year. Then I forgot about him because I always had such a lot of homework to do all the time.

It was in the summer vacation after my freshman year that I had that dream about Clifford. And it was when school started again that Johnnie came into the library as I was sitting at Uncle Eric's big table and doing my homework, and he had the evening paper folded over which he put in front of me.

"Say, Bunny, wasn't this the kid that did not kiss you on your graduation night and you got so mad that you cried?"

I took the paper and read how "...a prominent attorney's son..." who had been treated for a length of time at a sanatorium for tuberculosis, had died.

"Poor Clifford," was all I could say, and then I told my dream to Johnnie, who marvelled at it.

Chapter 4

It was ages it seemed since the Senior Prom and almost a week since I saw Stephen on his roof. I lay in bed early this morning and tried to remember every single thing about him. After awhile, I got up and got dressed and thought that maybe I could go exploring down Benjamin Lane and I just might run into Stephen.

Aunt Cora was chatting away about what she would do today and I was only half listening because I was thinking how I could see Stephen again after I did my chores around the house. I decided that if I went walking down Benjamin Lane, it would look like I was hoping to see him. No, I could not do that.

It was when I was straightening up my room after breakfast when I heard Aunt Cora call that she was going out. And it got very quiet in the house. Uncle Eric was somewhere around but I did not know where. Bye and bye, I went into the library to find something to read and sat in Uncle Eric's huge chair which I swung around so I would get the light from the left and the back of the chair faced the hallway. Sitting like this nobody could see me from the hallway.

I don't know how long I had been reading when vaguely I heard Aunt Cora come back and I heard her talking to Uncle Eric in the dining room. Then I heard Aunt Cora's voice say real loud, "You don't say!"

And then Uncle Eric said, "I do not know quite what to do about the reply we received from Mr. Framingham's studio. After my initial rage, I simmered down enough to realize that they are probably right. He is a very famous and apparently, a very rich man, and probably has many claims made against him for fathering offspring. But, I really thought that I was very explicit regarding Bunny's relationship to him and cited all the facts regarding his parenthood which left no doubt about their authenticity. I quoted from documents, which, I said, were available for his examination. And I requested an interview at the earliest possible opportunity.

"Then to receive a set of forms to fill out from the studio requesting photos of the mother in the attire worn and style of hair arrangement identical with the time of the alleged intercourse which resulted in a pregnancy. They ask for date, time and place of the act. And they ask for birth details of the offspring—hospital, doctor, date, place, etc., etc. And then one must have all the forms notarized and returned.

"I swear, Cora, they never even read the letter I sent. They probably said, 'Here's another one of those letters — send forms so-and-so, and file this letter with the others like it.' I seriously doubt if Framingham even saw my letter, which his agent advised me to send to the studio when he wrote us that he no longer represented Framingham."

"I bet you're right," I heard Aunt Cora say.

"To tell you the truth, Cora, I am sick of the whole thing, and am tempted to forget about it and do nothing more. Now that we know that Bunny is a Pendleton legally, I see no point in continuing that frustrating business. It is apparent that Bunny's father must know that he has a daughter, because he must have had to sign some sort of paper to relinquish her for adoption. I do not know what to think at this stage, Cora."

"But what are we going to do?" Aunt Cora asked.

"I don't know, darling. I don't know."

And I heard them both go toward the back of the house.

Now I had something new to think about. It was not a nice thought. My own father thought so little of me that he never even tried to find me. After awhile I just gave up even as Uncle Eric did. I decided that if Aunt Cora and Uncle Eric asked me what I would like to do about getting in touch with my father, I would tell them to forget about it.

And I went back to thinking about Stephen again. I wasn't very much along in thinking about Stephen when the doorbell rang and pretty soon there was a loud, "Yoo, hoo!" Eda was at the door, so I sighed and got up to let her in.

Her grandmother must have given her the allowance because she had a bunch of movie magazines under her arm. Eda was always buying movie magazines and she was always crazy over somebody different, depending on which movie she saw last. She had to go to the Saturday matinee every week, so she changed her favorite actor and actress every week.

I went with her once in awhile but mostly I did not care much for anything connected with acting. I supposed it had something to do with my mother being killed in that accident a long time ago, and she having been an actress.

If I did not go with Eda to the movies on Saturday, she generally went to the drugstore after she got out of them and bought up all the movie magazines that she did not have already. And then she would come over to our house and sit in the gazebo when it was warm, or in our library when it was cold, and she would read the whole magazine—every word—and kiss the pictures of all the actors and actresses that she liked. I did not say anything, but I thought she was crazy to do that.

And this time she came in with more magazines. She started reading out loud how the new "talkies" were definitely going to get all the big stars of the "silents" fired because it took a different kind of acting to do the "talkies". I was only half listening when I heard the name of Vern Framingham and went over quickly to look at the article. It said that Vern Framingham did not have a good enough voice because of a New England twang which was nasal and which sounded terrible in the talkies. And that was the reason that his major studio had dropped him. And now his latest studio would not renew his contract, it was said. And the article said that he was working constantly with speech coaches to correct his accent. But there was doubt whether he would later ever make another picture.

Well, after that I went through all the other magazines to see what they had to say about my father.

When Eda finished the magazine that she was reading, she said, "Hey, let's go for a walk."

"Where?"

"Oh, just mess around."

"I have an idea," I said when it came to me how I could maybe see Stephen. "Let's go clear around my house. I have never done it."

"So let's," and Eda got up ready to go.

At our front gate we turned right and walked to the end of our fence which was at the corner of the avenue, and turned right again. We walked until we reached the end of our fence. Now, if anyone was in a hurry, they would miss the lane easily, because the sidewalk just went on without a break, although there was no curb and autos could drive in. On the other corner was a store with a sign over it, saying MEATS—GROCERIES—VARIETY. Prop. Pasco Guidice, was printed on the second line in smaller letters. Up over the store, one could see that originally it was a white Colonial house and that someone had made the first floor of it into a store. The upper part was still a beautiful house and it had a cupola on top. And at one time, it looked like the store had been painted white, but now everything was sort of a dingy light gray. On the side of the store was a weathered sign saying BENJAMIN LANE.

"That Pasco," Eda was saying, "is a mean and dirty old bastard."

"Eda!" I almost shrieked. "You can't use that kind of words!"

"Well, my mother calls him that!"

"I don't care. Maybe it's all right for grownups to use words like that, but not for us."

Eda went on. "He came around my mother before she married the captain, but you can bet your boots he didn't come to ask her to marry him—only to get what he could get without marrying."

"Eda! You shouldn't talk like that about your mother!"

"I'm not talking about my mother. I'm talking about him. He's a mean and stingy old bas— geezer. He never was married and he cheats everybody who buys in his store."

"How do you know?"

"Everybody says so. How else could he own the tenement house with nine families living there if he didn't cheat to get all that money?"

"Did he ever cheat you?"

"How could he? I never buy in his store."

"Then you have no right to say he's a cheat. He may be a lonely old man that nobody loves and that makes him look mean."

"Oh, you're such a goody two-shoes," she gave me a small shove.

By this time, we had walked on and stood facing the tenement building, which was three stories high and had three doorways, evenly spaced, opening onto the lane. We were leaning against the high board fence of my home and I knew that Stephen lived in one of the tenements on the opposite side. But which one?

"Do you know anyone who lives there?" I asked Eda, sort of

casual like.

"Nope." And she went on. I followed her.

At the end of my fence was a white low picket fence around a tidy looking garden with a wonderful lot of flowers of all colors and a nice smell of them. Eda leaned way over to get a good whiff.

"Gee, this garden smells most as good as yours."

"Your English is terrible, Eda."

"Yeah, I know." She did not sound worried at all. In fact, she was smiling. "Hey! There's even a pump in there! Just like in your garden."

Right then a lady popped up from where she had been kneeling among some tall bushes. She was wearing an old-fashioned sunbonnet and had on a dirty old pair of gloves.

"Would you girls like to come in and see the whole garden and enjoy it? I'm really proud of it. And would you like some cookies and lemonade?"

Before I could say, "No, thank you," or "Yes, thank you," Eda had already said, "You betcha!" and had the gate open and walked right in. I had to follow her.

"Boy! You have such beautiful flowers," she was saying, "and I just love cookies and lemonade."

I studied the lady as she told us the names of the flowers, both in Latin and in English, so I guessed that maybe she was a teacher because she spoke very good English like Uncle Eric and Johnnie. And I was right because she told us that she had the second grade in the primary school on the other side of the avenue. She wanted to know where we went when we were in primary school, but before we could answer, an old lady came out on the porch to see what the talking was all about. So we got introduced and their name was Grant. The old lady was the teacher's mother, who was so glad to have us for company. They both knew who Uncle Eric was and knew right away that I was their neighbor.

We sat on the front porch and ate yummy raisin cookies and drank cold lemonade with chunks of ice in it. Miss Grant told us that the great tasting lemonade was made with the spring water from the pump in the garden. And then I found out that Stephen lived in the middle part of the tenement house, on the second floor.

It was when I asked if they knew any of the people living in the lane that the teacher's mother told us that they knew everybody. They told us that they were living on the street even before Pasco Guidice bought the corner house and made it into a market. And then he had the tenement house built some time later, on the land that came with the corner house. As they were talking, you could see that they were not at all happy about the grocer, and the tenement house.

So I said that we were going to walk clear around my house and that is how we happened to be in the lane. And they said that we could not do that because Ben's shop made the lane into a dead-end street. Ben, the cobbler, had a tiny basement cobbler shop and lived in back of it while the rest of his house was shut off and empty.

"Sounds spooky!" said Eda and she jumped up. "Let's go see!"

Miss Grant jumped up, too. "I'll go with you and introduce you to Ben."

Something in her voice made me look at her quickly. I think that only I was aware of her sounding excited, and her cheeks got pinker.

"Should you, dear?" asked her mother and I could hear a little sharp edge to her voice.

Miss Grant did not say anything, but her manner changed after we left her porch and started walking toward the end of the lane. She even seemed to get a little giggly, but in a nice grownup way. And we had to walk quickly to keep up with her. By the manner of how she lifted her shoulder a little and how her lips tightened after her mother asked if she should go, I guessed that there was something about the cobbler that the mother didn't like.

And then I felt as if there were strings inside of me that were tightening like a violin being tuned. Maybe I would hear and see and sense more than was on the surface pretty soon and I was being adjusted to receive the impressions.

So Miss Grant walked between Eda and me and when we got to the end of the lane, we walked along a short pathway and down three steps from the little entry inside the door, into a basement cobbler shop. A large store window had been put in that gave a whole view of the lane right up to the avenue, so the shop was very light.

As we came in, a very tall man wearing a leather apron got up from where he was putting a new sole on a shoe, and came toward us. He had thick wavy hair of a black and gray mixture, and a smiling look on his face, yet his lips were not smiling. But his eyes were the most looking-deep-into-you kind of eyes I ever saw, and they were such kind eyes of a very deep blue color. He shook hands with Eda and me and bowed a little when Miss Grant introduced him to us. And then Miss Grant told him that I lived in the big house in back of her house and Eda was my friend, and that we were exploring the neighborhood, so she thought she would introduce him to us in the event we wanted any shoes fixed sometime.

He smiled and it was a wonderful smile, and he asked us if we would have some coffee and some biscuits that he himself had baked that morning.

Eda was staring at him and being speechless for once, for this was no ordinary cobbler. He brought in the coffee pot and the cups and saucers as well as the biscuits, butter and marmalade.

Then he said, "Yes, indeed, I, myself, am quite impressed with my own culinary expertise. I would make some deserving lady a very fine husband."

I sensed rather than heard Miss Grant catch her breath, and it suddenly dawned on me that Miss Grant must be sweet on Ben and that he was sweet on her, but her mother didn't like it.

"By the way," she said quickly as if to change the subject, "do you know anything historical about our little street that you can tell the girls?"

"Indeed I do. Actually, in the beginning, it was not a street at all. It was a long driveway from the main road and this house was an inn way back in the latter 1700's and early 1800's. The inn provided overnight lodging for travelers and a stable to rest and feed their horses. The owner of the inn was Benjamin Lane, in fact, an ancestor of mine. Here, wait a minute. I have the original sign that used to swing on a hinge fastened to a pole not far from this spot. The family held onto the sign from generation to generation."

He got up and went to the back of the shop and after rummaging around, came carrying a very old weather-beaten wooden plank on which one could still see a faint picture of a chaise being drawn by two horses, and still make out in large letters BENJAMIN LANEs INN.

"I didn't know about this," said Miss Grant wonderingly as we all crowded around to look at the old sign.

"Gee! That's more than a hundred years old," said Eda.

"Indeed it is," said the cobbler. Then he went on. "It seems that in those days a secret fraternity was flourishing, which was dedicated to bettering the lot of mankind, and there are oblique references here and there in obscure publications that some of our founding fathers in this nation belonged to this fraternity. And it seems that there were branches of this fraternity in Europe, which may explain why foreigners like Lafayette, Kosciusko and Pulaski, all members of this fraternity, came to join the Colonies in their struggle to form a new nation based on principles heretofore not manifested anywhere. And then, of course, there followed the French Revolution and the unsuccessful Polish uprising. In any event, the meeting places for this fraternity were sometimes in private homes, but, most often in inns similar to Benjamin Lane's. In my family it was said that there was such a meeting place in Providence and it would not surprise me a bit if it were at this very inn."

Well, none of us said anything. It was such a big thing to soak up.

And after awhile Ben went on. "Prior to the Civil War and during it, there was underground traffic in runaway slaves, with several stations in New England. It was a highly secret operation, you may be sure. It is said that there still are a few underground passages between some of the old houses even in Providence, and perhaps Benjamin Lane's old inn may have been such a way station. Who can tell?"

As I sat and listened to Ben, I had the feeling that he was telling us only a tiny bit of what he really knew. I felt that he knew an awful lot about the secret fraternity, or else why did he even mention it? Somewhere the American Revolution had to be planned and it had to be all over the Colonies, in order for it to be successful.

And then the cobbler seemed to be talking only to Miss Grant when he said, "One could not always tell by a man's outer occupation, no matter how lowly, what his real status in life was. A printer, an innkeeper, a farmer, a cobbler, could actually have been a very important person whose endeavors had far-reaching effects."

I knew then that he was telling her that his being only a cobbler did not prove that he was not a more important person.

For a bit, I forgot about Stephen, but remembered when we were back outside and walking toward Miss Grant's little house. Her mother was standing at the gate and waiting for us.

Eda and I did not continue our walk around the house, but went back to my yard to sit in the gazebo.

More than anything I wanted to talk to somebody on how I felt about Stephen, but knew that I could not say anything to Eda because it was impossible for her to keep a secret. I felt miserable and it must have showed.

"You look mopey," she said. "Don't you feel good?"

The only thing I could think of at the moment of what made me a little mad at Eda, was the subject of homework. I knew that sometime this summer, I had to tell her that I would not be helping her with her homework as much next year when we were both seniors. It was bad enough when we were freshmen and sophomores, but when we got to be juniors, it got worse than ever. I had all I could do to keep up with my own school work, never mind doing all the research for her papers, too.

And it was all because word got around that I was John Pendleton's sister. I suppose one teacher told another and they all knew who he was and some of them even asked me how things were with Johnnie and what he was doing. Well, they expected smartness to run in the family, and I really had to push myself from practically the very first day I went to high school. Actually, most of the time I did not feel like studying, but realized that I had no choice as a matter of fact, and owed it to the family to get the best marks possible. Of course, I always got the right answers when I concentrated very hard, but that was not good enough. I had to work everything out correctly to arrive at the right answer, and this was harder to do than not knowing the answer at all.

Here is when I missed Percy most of all. He used to help me with my homework all the time. For a time after I started going to high school, and when I was in the house alone, I used to go from room to room calling Percy. But the house was empty. Gradually, by Christmas time, I had to accept the fact that Percy was no longer with us. I missed him very much. And I was very sorry that I had a fight with him and I asked God's forgiveness and asked Him to give a message to Percy about my being very sorry that I said anything to hurt his feelings and that I was apologizing.

So, having to do all the homework all by myself with no Percy to help me and studying to keep up the honor of the Pendleton name, I had no time for anything else. With all that studying and doing extra assignments and writing reports, I missed out on all the extracurricular activities that were fun. But the only thing I did get in on was the music and that was only because they always wanted me to play the piano. And that was no fun but a lot of work, too. So I missed out on a lot of fun that was going on. I had no time to go to any games or join any clubs, because it took all my spare time to keep up with my school work. Besides, I simply was not born smart. I had to work at it, and it took all my time. And then I got stuck with helping Eda with her homework.

It all began about a month after we started high school when everybody got to know who I was because of Johnnie, and Eda went around bragging that I was her best friend. I discovered very soon how that led to my having to help her with her school work. With me not being smart at all, she was worse. In fact, she was almost dumb in school. Anyway, she used to save up her homework for Saturday and would bring it along after she got out of the movies and brought all the magazines along for me to look through, because that was the only way I could get to read about my father. Naturally, nobody guessed this.

As if that was not enough, Aunt Cora was doing homework, too. It was her idea and Uncle Eric planned a whole course of study for her in English composition, grammar, reading, and history. She felt funny about asking questions of Uncle Eric or Johnnie, so she asked me instead. I looked her compositions over, listened to her read, and reviewed her answers on her homework assignments. The huge table in the library was hardly big enough for all the work papers from Aunt Cora, Eda and me.

Of all the useless things I had to waste my time on at school, I thought that gym was the best example. And the gym clothes we wore were ridiculous, too. Aunt Cora and I went downtown to buy them right after I went to high school. We had to have dark blue serge pleated bloomers that came down over the knees, black cotton stockings, and sneakers. A white middy blouse with a sailor collar and a long black sailor tie completed the outfit. I had to try everything on and felt sort of swallowed up because Aunt Cora bought everything a couple of sizes too big, so the outfit would last for four years and I would grow into it.

I felt that I got all the exercise I needed by walking back and forth between the house and the school every day. I also did my chores around the house every day, because Aunt Cora said it was good for one's character to work no matter how rich one was.

Well, in the end I did not really mind gym that much even if it did bore me, and was a waste of time for me. But Eda was wild about it. She liked gym so much that the gym teacher made her a leader. Pretty soon she was on the basketball team, and all the other teams and a cheer leader, and had to stay after school for practice. But, in order to stay on the teams and be a cheer leader and keep up the honor of the school, she had to keep her grades up. Nobody else she knew could help her, because she did not know any other "grinds"—people who studied all the time—so I got stuck with helping her, too. Besides, she used to bring all those movie magazines when she came over, and I couldn't tell her that I wouldn't help her with her homework when I wanted to read everything I could find about my father. Reading things like he sold his big beautiful house, and then he sold his polo ponies and then his Rolls Royce. In one of the articles, he said that the talkies were just a novelty which would pass, and that the talkies could never replace the silents.

Then he got married to the big star Norma Hightower, who also said that the talkies would never replace the silents.

Every time Eda brought the magazines, there was something about my father in them, so I just had to keep on reading them. Later on, his and his new wife's contracts were not renewed. And then there was the news everywhere that Norma Hightower divorced him and took practically all his money. Another time it said that he signed with a smaller studio that was experimenting with talkies, and then the studio cancelled his contract just like the major one did before. Then there were no more mentions about him.

While I was thinking all this, Eda did not wait for me to tell her why I was mopey, but started talking about Clifford dying. I wished she wouldn't talk about poor Clifford. She did not really know him at all, but the way she talked, you would think that they were the best of friends.

The funniest thing was that she actually believed all the things she said even if they were not true. I guessed to myself that if I studied her most carefully—how she acted and how she talked—I would know most of the people in the world and how they were. Sometimes when she came over, she would chatter away—talk, talk, talk—and when she went away, she would not even realize, I bet, that I had not said one single word in all the time she had been around me.

But, I learned a lot from her, too. I learned what was going on at school. I was so busy studying and looking things up and writing reports that I had no time for listening to everybody. But, Eda was all wrapped up in everything going on, so she kept me informed.

I interrupted her while she was talking about Clifford. "Wait up, Eda, I want you to listen because I'm going to tell you something you may not like about when we go back to school in September."

"Yeah?"

I had her attention. "It's like this. I will not be able to help you with your homework like I did all of last year and the other years before that. You must admit that you had a wonderful time running around to all the games and being in dramatics and all kinds of fun, while all the time I was the one that was looking things up for you both in the school library and in the public library and in Uncle Eric's library in all my spare time and after school. I corrected your themes and spelling and went over your algebra problems with you, and I even carried your books home when you had practice in gym or were rehearsing in dramatics after school.

"You took a lot of advantage of me when I had to do my own homework, too. You must remember that I had to do my own homework after I got finished helping you with yours. Ever since we were freshmen, our classes have not been the same. You always had different homework from mine."

"Can I help it if you're a brain!" Eda yelled. "You're supposed to be my best friend, Thelma! How can you talk like that? Besides you are in the smart division and I'm in the dumb one because I'm not as smart as you are. So any little help you give me with my homework is no big thing to you. You're just being mean, that's what!" And she started to cry.

I tried to put my arm around her shoulders, but she shook it off and ran out of the gazebo, down the path to the gate and off to her grandmother's, I supposed.

All I could do was make a big sigh. Eda could never understand any other side but her own.

I knew that she would be back in a couple of days because of her crush on Johnnie, and I wasn't looking forward to telling her that Johnnie decided to go to San Francisco and learn all about Uncle Eric's ship business and all.

Then I remembered that her mother lived in San Francisco and maybe she would want to move there, too, in order to have better chances to see Johnnie. The thought cheered me a little at getting rid of her and the next minute I felt I was being mean. But, gee whiz! She could be such a pest. So I went inside to play a little on the piano.

With all the hard work when I first got into high school, I still found at least an hour a day for my piano practice. Of course, I did not play all summer last year because I was away at Eda's grandmother's summer cottage at Rocky Point, but I started in again as soon as I was back. In getting my hour of practice done, I used to play at all hours of the day and evening when I had a little time. The habit was so deep, that if I went to bed without practicing, I could not sleep. I had to get up, go downstairs and get that practicing done.

Another thing that kept me from sleeping sometimes, was not finishing a chord. There were many times that I got up again after

I had gone to bed and went downstairs to bang the piano once, then come up again and get into bed so I could get to sleep. I guessed that everybody had their odd peculiarities about them, so I really could not be too critical of Eda.

In the end, I got to liking to play the piano even though it was work. It was relaxing when I was all tensed up and nervous from studying. Of course, I no longer had to think which finger to use in order to play which note. Still, playing the piano did not come easily to me, either. I had to work hard at it as well, like everything else.

Somehow I got through the first three years in high school in spite of myself. I had to push myself all the time to get the A's and maybe one or two B's. One B was always in gym, which did not count, after all. Everybody at home was happy about my report cards and that counted. So I didn't care about the B in gym.

It must be getting to lunch time, I thought to myself while I was playing when I heard Johnnie whistling as he came in from his "digs" as he called the rooms fixed up for him in the carriage house.

And then I heard somebody running up the driveway and around to the living room entrance where I was playing. It was Eda who ran in through the doors that I had left open because it was so nice and warm outside and I liked to hear the birds sing and they got loud every time I played. She plunked herself beside me on the bench and kept blowing her nose and wiping her eyes.

Oh, my goodness, I thought to myself. What's the matter now. It must be a new catastrophe bigger than my not wanting to do her homework because she would have waited to come back on that one. So I hurried up and finished my piece to hear what she had to tell me.

"Johnnie is going to San Francisco. Far away to San Francisco!" she informed me in tragic tones as if the end of the world had come.

I was relieved that I did not have to tell her about his leaving after all, but then wondered how she knew.

She told me. "My grandmother just got a letter from my mother and she wrote that the captain told her about Johnnie's coming out and making a few trips on the ship so he could learn the sailing part of the lumber business. Then Johnnie is going to work in San Francisco at the office."

"So what's there to cry about?" I asked as if I didn't know.

She looked at me a long time out of red and swollen eyes. And I could sense the minute she decided to tell me.

"I'm going to let you in on a deep dark secret but you must promise, cross your heart, and hope to die that you will never tell."

So I did.

And she said, "I am madly in love with Johnnie and I have been for a long, long time."

Well, I couldn't act surprised even to satisfy her so I decided to make believe that I did not believe her.

"And I'm going to marry him some day," she finished before I could say anything. "So I don't know what I'll do if I can't see him practically every day. I'll just die!"

"Oh, go on! What about all those actors you're so crazy about?"

"That's different. That's not for real."

"You certainly don't act like it isn't for real. Hugging and kissing all those actors' pictures in the movie magazines."

"Well, that's not loving them like I'm gonna marry them!" and she started to cry again.

"Oh," I said and wondered if I was in love with Stephen like I wanted to marry him. And that was something I had to think more about later. Right now I pulled my mind back to Eda on how to stop her crying.

"Maybe Johnnie will stay at your mother's when he's going to the office in San Francisco. So it won't be like he's going out of your life forever, Eda."

The sun came out again for her, and she jumped up. "I'm gonna write my mother and ask her if I can move to San Francisco right away!" She hugged me and ran off again.

❖❖❖

Chapter 5

I woke up suddenly and lay listening. There was still an echo of a bell's ringing in my ears, but the bell tone did not come again. Instead, after awhile as I lay listening, I seemed to hear way inside of me as if I were talking to myself:

In 1756 the custom was to christen newborn children in the Lane family—

And then the sentence died away. I opened my eyes, shut them again, and listened some more, but nothing came. So, I lay and wondered if Eda had written her mother as she said she would. I wondered, also, if she would want to give up all those athletic activities that she was into at school, which she would have to do if she moved to San Francisco. Even as a freshman, she made her mark at gym. The difference between her and me showed up so strongly at Final Assembly when the prizes, letters and recognitions were passed out. I always got the scholastic prizes, certificates and things, while Eda got all the athletic ones. I just knew that she would be the captain of all the girls' teams going when she got to be a senior and maybe even before. And she always boasted everywhere that I was her best friend and that I was the smartest one in the whole school. Oh, dear, how I hoped it were true.

Then I got up and decided I would go up to my hideaway in back of the chimney and look through the telescope that Johnnie gave me and maybe I would see Stephen up on the roof of his house.

So right after breakfast and after doing all my chores, I went up to the attic and looked to the roof of the block where Stephen lived. There were some clothes hanging on the line but what caught my attention was a man doing gymnastics. He was waving his arms and bending and kicking his legs, and doing deep knee bends and all sorts of other exercises. All of a sudden, he dropped down and sat with his back to the chimney and with his legs stretched out in front of him. The door opened in the boxlike structure on the roof and a lady came out carrying a basket. She said something to the man and he waved his hand while she started taking the clothes down and putting them in the basket. After she was done, she talked some more to the man, and then picked up the basket and went away.

The man sat still for a bit, then got up slowly again and did some more gymnastics—really hard ones like he was trying to get good and tired.

I must have watched him at least an hour. Then, he went on tiptoe to the door and sat down. He started pushing himself first on one side then on the other and got himself over the door sill and I saw him gradually slide down the stairs in a sitting position. He reached in back of him and pushed the door shut and I could not see him any more.

Seeing all this set me to thinking real hard. It looked like the man was pretending to be lame. And Stephen had said that his father got hurt at a factory and could not walk. My heart started pounding real hard and I could not think what I should do. It was awful. I couldn't imagine Stephen would lie about his father. And I remembered how Stephen said that his father was on half-pay, and in a way his lameness was a blessing because if he had been working, he would have been laid off and they would have no money coming in. This was so awful that I wished I had never seen it.

I was sitting on the floor and thinking all those awful thoughts when I heard a loud "Yoo-hoo!" outside downstairs, so I got up and went down to see what was new with Eda.

Aunt Cora had let her in and she was coming up the stairs when I met her as I was going down. She wanted to go for a walk. I suggested downtown with a stop at the library. I had to get Johnnie aside and tell him what I had seen on Stephen's roof and ask him what I should do.

Well, it was almost lunch time so Eda's face lit up because Johnnie always bought us ice cream cones when we went to see him around noon. Besides which, we always rode in his roadster to the ice cream place on Arthur Avenue and Eda got to sitting next to him. My being in love with Stephen made me understand now how Eda grabbed every chance to see Johnnie and every little bit helped.

The mystery to me was how Johnnie seemed totally unaware of all this and just walked around with his head in the clouds. He was so busy studying and reading and researching that he even did not run around after Pembroke girls that some of the Brown guys always talked about when they came to see Johnnie. Whenever there was something coming up like a dance or something like that and Johnnie needed to take a girl to, he always did not have one at the last minute. So Aunt Cora would help out by making me up and helping me to dress up so I would look older and I would go with him. He always asked me as a big favor and I couldn't say, "No."

Anyway, Eda and I walked to the library and when we got there we leaned against the parapet in the sunshine at the top of the steps in front of the library doors, because Johnnie always came out front at lunch time in the event that I might be there.

Oh, my! I almost fainted when he came out with Stephen! They were laughing and Johnnie explained to us girls that he had called the high school office and listed the open job at the public library at the time when he decided that he would go to San Francisco to work for Uncle Eric. He had taken the library job after he graduated from Brown only until a replacement could be found. Meanwhile, Stephen went to the high school to check on any job openings and grabbed the job in the library. While all this explanation was going on, I could only look at Stephen. He smiled nicely at me and shook my hand. Then I turned to introduce him to Eda. Of course, she knew who he was but I did not know whether she had met him or not.

He turned to her and held out his hand. Then, a funny thing happened. She put her hand in his and they became like two persons in a dream. They didn't say, "How do you do," or anything like that, either. They just stood there, looking at each other and holding hands, like two statues.

The tears rushed up to my eyes and I did not know why. I turned away just as Johnnie said real low into my ear, "Ho! Ho! Looks like love at first sight, by gosh!"

Then real loud, "Hey, you two! Let's get going! We haven't all afternoon."

He opened the rumble seat for them when we got to the Empire Street side where the roadster was parked, and they got in, still without saying a word.

By then I was so mad at Eda, I could have slapped her. I was more than mad. I was furious. They were very quiet in back and I didn't dare turn around because I didn't want anybody to see my face. I was heartbroken and angry and very jealous all at the same time. I wanted to cry and scream and beat with my fists, but had to sit still as if there was absolutely nothing different going on.

After we got to the ice cream place, Johnnie asked me, "Anything the matter, Bunny?"

I shook my head.

"Everybody is so quiet all of a sudden," said Johnnie. "Who wants what on the cones?"

"Chocolate!" Eda said.

"Same for me," I heard Stephen say.

"Maple walnut," I managed without bursting out crying.

"Back in a jiffy," Johnnie ran into the store and I followed him. I could not stand being in the same place with those two. By now, I was very, very angry.

At the same time I was surprised at myself that I could actually enjoy the ice cream cone even with my broken heart. While I ate I decided that I would get even with Stephen by telling everybody what a great big fat old fake his father is. And that would make Eda sorry, too, I hoped. And Stephen would be sorry, as well, that he toyed with my affections.

Eda was very quiet on our way back home. In fact, she did not say anything to me all the way back to the corner of my street. I said to her very coldly, "I have a headache and I'm going to lie down when I get home and I don't feel like having any company."

For once, she did not run after me or give me any arguments. She just turned to cross the street and went on to her grandmother's.

And I went up to my room as soon as I got home without even looking for Aunt Cora. I lay across the bed and cried and cried and cried until I fell asleep.

Three things woke me up. I heard the echo of a bell and this was followed by:

In 1756 the custom was to christen newborn
children in the Lane family—

And I heard a knock on the door.

"Yes?" I called sleepily.

Johnnie stuck his head inside the door. "Dinner's ready. Aunt Cora asked me to wake you up. She had looked in on you earlier but you were fast asleep. You better get up or you will not want to sleep all night."

"O.K." I said and went into the bathroom to wash my face in cold water. My eyes still looked a little swollen but it only gave me a sleepy look, not like I had been crying a lot.

After dinner Johnnie said, "Well, I got a replacement at the library. You'd never guess who it is, Uncle Eric. It's the kid who took Bunny to his high school Senior Prom. Remember him?"

"Is that a fact!" Uncle Eric was surprised.

"Sure is. I trained him all day today, so he can take over tomorrow. It is only putting books away, so the girls who shack for them can show him where a book goes if he forgets about the different collections. He is taking the job only temporarily, anyway, he told me. The company where his father was disabled, promised to call him whenever a vacancy occurs. But, with times like they are, who knows when that will be. They will want experienced people first."

"He is lucky to get even that much," Uncle Eric agreed.

"So I will start going through my stuff tonight and put aside the things I want to take when I leave for San Francisco.

"Hey, Bunny! Want to come help me after you finish helping Aunt Cora with the dishes?"

"It's all right, dear," Aunt Cora said. "You go right ahead. I will do the dishes myself."

"No, fair lady! Light o' my love! Love of my life! I will do the dishes while you whisper sweet nothings— No! That's not right! Sweet somethings into mine ear— Who knows? I may never get to finishing the dishes because I will carry you off to my lair!" Once in awhile, Uncle Eric would talk like Shakespeare. He now waved his arm toward the stairway, and Aunt Cora jumped up to go sit on his lap.

"Is that a promise?" she laughed.

I almost started to cry again, but Johnnie grabbed my arm and pulled me out the door. He was chuckling to himself and shaking his head, while I was fighting away another flood of tears.

Once at Johnnie's place, he pushed me into an armchair and sat on the floor in front of me.

"What's bothering you, Bunny? You have not been yourself in quite awhile. Come on! You can tell me. Maybe I can help."

I didn't know what to say. I didn't want to tell him about falling in love with Stephen and getting jealous of Eda. And I didn't know how to begin telling him about Stephen's father. Johnnie kept sitting there and staring at me, so I had to say something.

"Yes. Something funny peculiar has been happening," I began. "It happens just when I wake up. In fact, it wakes me up. I hear a bell. No, that's not it exactly. It is as if a bell, or a gong, had been struck somewhere, and I am only hearing the echo of it—the reverberation.

"And then I hear inside of me, 'In 1756 the custom was to christen newborn children in the Lane family—', and then everything fades away. It is my own voice that is saying this, Johnnie. And I don't know what the idea of it all is."

Johnnie got up and walked around a bit. He patted the back of his head and whistled through his teeth. And then he said, "I seem to recall reading somewhere—I think it was in someone's autobiography— Some poet, I think, and—er—it seems that is the way his work was written. He would hear it inside of himself and then he would write it. So, why don't you try it, Bunny? Next time you hear this, write down what you are hearing."

"I'm scared, Johnnie. Maybe I'm beginning to hear voices and I'm going crazy."

"I don't think so. As a matter of fact, I think you are more of what a human being is supposed to be, more than the rest of us insensitive clods. If God created mankind in His image, it stands to reason that some speck of His attributes should surface somewhere in someone, once in awhile. Mankind was created as God's supreme effort in order to rule over all of creation. What happened to mankind?" By now Johnnie was talking more to himself than to me.

"What's that got to do with me?" I asked.

"That's just it, Bunny. You are more attuned to what is really going on out there where past, present, and future is ever the eternal now. Maybe you are not attuned perfectly, but are more so than the rest of us. So you may be hearing something out of the past which affects your life in some way. Maybe you are more like the human being that God created and meant humanity to be like."

"You really think that I should write down what I hear?"

"I would. If my inner self went to all the trouble of telling me something, I sure would make a note of it."

I'll try it and see what happens."

So we went back to the house without my helping Johnnie sort things out and packing, and I did not say anything about Stephen's father, either. Somehow, I just couldn't.

Aunt Cora and Uncle Eric were being very noisy out in the kitchen, laughing and joking, when we came in through the kitchen door.

Uncle Eric snapped his fingers as if he remembered something and said to me, "I have been meaning to have a little talk with you about your future, Bunny. You are going into the last year of high school, and I was wondering if you had any special field of interest that you may want to go into more deeply. We have to start thinking of which college you want to go to when you graduate from high school."

It was funny that Uncle Eric should bring up the subject because I had been thinking about it, too. I did not really want to go to any kind of a school any more. I could hardly wait to finish high school.

Once in awhile I used to think what I wanted to be when I grew up, but none of the subjects I ever studied really interested me. I read everything I had to and did all the homework assignments, but I only did it because I was supposed to and not because I liked any of it.

"Why do we have to study all the things we do at school? What use is it to us?" I now asked Uncle Eric.

And he said, "It is mental discipline, Bunny, for the most part. We train our brains to work at their best. Each one of us living on this earth has to do something with his life whether he likes it or not. And the only equipment we have is our brains and our skills. While we are at school, we study all the things that have gone on before, so that we can pick up where the others left off and go on from there in some field or another. Do you see?"

"I guess so. But I don't know what I want to do."

He put his head to one side and stared at me. Then, he said, "Personally I do not believe that there is one person on this whole terrestrial globe, who is not of use somewhere in some way in the vast scheme of things. Some may have a very small place of little importance, nevertheless they must fulfill their function.

"Don't worry about it, dear. It is bound to come to you eventually where your place is, I feel sure. It may even be that you have a special place. For the present, we may enter you at Pembroke," he said.

I shuddered inwardly. I did not want to go to Pembroke. "Well, I'm getting pretty good on the piano," I said hopefully.

"That's good! That's good. Keep it up. Each skill you acquire is not carried on your back like a load. It may actually lighten the burden of life."

When I went upstairs, I started thinking some more about my piano playing. I did not feel that I was making that much fantastic progress, but I suppose I was, because it got easier for me to play real hard pieces. And Uncle Eric had started me on developing a technique so that I was not merely playing pieces but making music. Sometimes I argued with him about how a piece ought to be played. He would show me the expression marks and I would tell him that it was not the way I heard it in my head. When he got tired of arguing with me, he would go to the library and find the piece just exactly how it was written by the composer and not how it was arranged by somebody else and then he would get excited and get me to play the piece my way while he followed the score as the composer wrote it.

"Amazing! Incredible!" he would say to himself.

And when I got into bed later on, I put a notebook and a pencil on the stand near my bed in case I heard some more about the newborn children being christened.

Before I fell asleep, I started feeling that I was no longer a little girl and that I was on the way to being a grownup. Somehow, this day, I had reached the dividing line between childhood and youth. It made me very sad.

Chapter 6

When I woke up at the sound of the echo of a chime, and heard again the sentence starting, I put on the light and started in to write:

> In 1756 the custom was to christen newborn children in the Lane family. This event immediately brought forth the pastor and midwife from their beds at the insistent clamour of an urgent fist which broke in upon the fat slumbers of the usually fat pair of welcomers to the newly born human. Such was the welcome accorded the red wrinkled scion of the house of Lane. In truth it might be said that these two officials were the only ones eagerly ministering to the tasks incident to the advent of yet another addition to the population of the community.
>
> The father did not even know when his son was born and did not care to enquire for the details caused in this important event. The black man who attended Benjamin Lane, Senior, and acted as valet, butler, general supervisor, as well as informer in the Lane household, told his master of this event.
>
> "Have her—", the elder Lane stopped and grinned.
>
> The black man grinned. The master chuckled. His echo chuckled. And when the white man threw back his head and roared with laughter, the black man did likewise. The imitation stopped when the master suddenly stopped.
>
> The outburst was caused by the ineptitude of the remark Lane almost made. These morning, or rather mid-morning reports of news, delinquencies or infractions on the part of the slaves, were invariably followed by, "Have him (or her) punished," spoken by the master.
>
> This state of affairs made the black informer the most hated and feared man on the estates. It also made Lane, Senior, the most informed man in the county which also made him a man of esteem. His nature was too mild to have him feared. Another man as well informed would have become the

most powerful man in the community. Lane was much too lazy to bother. But his faithful servitor developed extraordinary powers of observation and deduction in the process of accumulating any and all sorts of information mostly incriminatory.

When Mose informed his master that he had an heir, the latter subconsciously resented it and started making the usual remark which displayed his displeasure. The event awakened in him memories of another event which had occurred in his youth and which still haunted him at intervals.

The mother of the heir was resentful at this curtailment of her activities. She had not the slightest interest at the miracle of her being able to bring forth a live human being. Nearly every woman is faced with this wonderment, but not Elvira Lane. She resented the swelling of her body and this pain. All she wanted was to be rid of the burden once and for all.

The only other person in any way interested in the advent of Benjamin Lane, Junior, into the world of matter, was a little black boy, who was told that he would have to "mind" the child and it would be his master.

The little black boy had no name. Someone omitted having him christened. They forgot who bore him and he was brought up by everybody amid blows and kicks. The little boy ran everybody's errands and performed all the mean tasks of the household. He slept anywhere and ate whenever and wherever he could get food. The one ambition of his life was to "belong" to someone. When Mose fell over him in the hall where he was sleeping, the boy shrank back from the expected blows. Mose lifted his hand from force of habit to hit the morsel of shrinking skin and bones in his grasp, when the thought occurred to him that the new addition of the family should have a "boy". He was much too busy to search for a "boy" and here was one in his grip. Providence is wonderful, he grinned at the thought.

"Yuh be new marster's bo'!" he pushed the boy from him.

The Negro child scrambled up and streaked up the stairs to halt outside the door of his "Master". His little heart beat so loudly and so joyously, it nearly jumped out of his frail but tough little body. At last he belonged.

The last sentence faded out in a whisper. The large clock downstairs struck the half-hour and I sat wondering what time it was. I could see that it was the middle of the night. I put out my light and went to sit on the window seat and to think about the grownup story that came to me. I had no difficulty in putting it all down as I heard it. The words came sometimes slowly and sometimes a little faster, like when someone dictates and goes only fast enough for the writer to keep up with the dictation.

I must have been cogitating for a half hour because I then heard the clock strike four and went back to bed. When I woke up again, it was the middle of the morning and I felt at peace.

I heard Eda's voice downstairs and then Aunt Cora's. The memory of Stephen came sharply back, but to my surprise, there was no ache in my heart. I guessed that I had cried it all out of myself last night.

Pretty soon I heard someone run up the stairs and Eda ran in. "Oh, you lazy bones! Come on and get up! I want to go to the library. It's most eleven o'clock."

"What do you want to go to the library for?"

"To see Stephen, of course. We're in love."

I rolled over and propped my chin up on my hand. "I thought you had a crush on Johnnie."

"So did I. But this is different. I looked at him and he looked at me and something happened."

"What would you do if another girl came along and took him away from you?"

"I'd kill her."

"You wouldn't."

"I would so."

"You're crazy."

"Yeah! About Stephen."

"Did you tell your grandmother?"

"Of course not. Think I'm crazy? She'd pack me off to my mother's so fast you couldn't see for dust."

"She would? Why?"

"She wouldn't want me to get a baby."

"Eda!" I shrieked.

She really shocked me. Of course, I knew all about babies because Aunt Cora told me way back when I first got my period and ran scared to tell her. She first slapped me very gently so I wouldn't get dark circles under my eyes when I got my period again every month. She told me that's what you're supposed to do when you are the first one that a girl having a period for the first time tells it to. She told me this right away so I wouldn't feel badly that she slapped me a little on my cheek. Then, she kissed me and explained how babies came. And she said how you have to get married first.

I jumped out of bed and shook Eda. "Are you planning to get married? Eda, you will not be sixteen until August! You can't get married until you're eighteen."

"Who says I can't? I can run away and lie about how old I am."

"Well I don't think that Stephen is that stupid."

"Oh, come on, Thelma, get dressed. I want to go to the library."

"Well, you have to go by yourself, because I got other things to do that are more important."

"What's more important than my happiness?"

"Mine."

"You're just an old meanie!" And she ran out of the house.

While I was having breakfast, I said to Aunt Cora, "Did you know that we have a small street at the back of our house, Aunt Cora?"

"We do?"

"Captain Olafsen never took down the wooden fence along the back part of our house, so you can't see the street. And there are tall bushes between the iron fence and the wooden one, so you can't get out there anyhow."

"I see," she said absent-mindedly.

"Eda and I decided to walk around the block and we turned right instead of left, like we always did at our gate, and we came to a sort of alley with a grocery store on the other side. So we turned in and next to the grocery store, there is a big brick house where nine families live. And beyond our fence, on this side, is a small house where a teacher and her mother live. And at the end, there is a house that's shut up and a cobbler has a shop in the cellar, and he lives in back of the shop."

"Well, what do you know!" Aunt Cora was still absent-minded and only half-listening to me.

"Do we have any shoes that need mending?"

Now, she gave me her whole attention. "What do you want to know for?"

"So I can take them to the cobbler," I explained.

"Oh, I dare say we do. Let me look. And to what cobbler are you going to take them?"

"I just finished telling you, Aunt Cora, about the cobbler in the alley down the other side of our house, in back."

"Oh, yes, so you did."

I had a bagful of shoes when I walked into the shop. There were two pairs of Johnnie's, a pair of Uncle Eric's, a pair of mine and two pairs of Aunt Cora's.

Ben lined them up on the counter and gave me a ticket for each pair.

So I said to him, "Can you tell me some more about this street and the inn that was here?"

He looked at me kind of sharp and asked, "What would you like to know?"

"Oh, I don't know— Something interesting like when was the inn built?"

"It was somewhere around the 1780's."

"Then it was built after the American Revolution."

"Yes. Actually, it was rebuilt then. The original one had burned down. The one that burned down had a different name."

"Oh!" At least I knew that it was not around in 1756, and that it was not Benjamin Lane's, but somebody else's. I had a funny feeling that the cobbler knew a whole lot more than he had told when Miss Grant, Eda and I visited his shop.

He turned away from me and did not pay any more attention to me as if I were not there while he started working on one of the shoes, so I left.

Miss Grant was in her garden again and she came to the fence as I was walking by, so I stopped.

"I just took some shoes to be fixed to the cobbler's and asked him to tell me some more about the inn, but he only said that it was rebuilt after the American Revolution after the first one burned down."

"Really? I did not know that it was not the original one. Actually, it is the side of the inn that faces the lane. The front of it faces the next street over. And the whole place is shuttered and closed. Ben Lane lives in back of his shop."

"Oh my!" I felt goose-pimply all over because I got that dictation this morning and it must have something to do with the cobbler's ancestors.

"Gee, you must know him a long time, Miss Grant."

"We went to school together. In fact he found a loose board in your fence a long time ago, and then he dug a crawl-through space under the iron fence and we used to get into your garden and explore all around."

We both laughed. She got a faraway look in her eyes and then some tears came and she turned away. More than anything I wanted to make her keep on talking. So I said right away quick, "Could you show me the loose board in the fence?"

She then sort of giggled and opened the gate for me. We went around her house to the back and there was our old fence. She leaned down and pulled at the bottom of a board and the whole thing came down. It was lucky that I was right in back of her and put my hands up to stop its falling on her back. Again we both started to laugh. The bushes were so thick that we could not get through but when I knelt down I could look through from underneath and still see a shallow dent off to the right under the rusted iron fence. All kinds of leaves and roots of the bushes had almost filled up the hole again. Mr. Olafsen had never done anything about cleaning up outside the iron fence way back of our house where it faced the lane.

"Lucille?" came Mrs. Grant's voice from the house.

"Yes, Mother!"

"Where are you?"

"Right here in the back yard."

"Is someone with you?"

"The little girl from the haunted house. Oh, my!" she clapped her hand over her mouth. "I'm sorry. It's what we used to call your house when we were children."

I started to giggle. "You did! We did, too, all us kids. So don't feel sorry. I used to get mad at kids when they called it that after we moved in, but not any more. It's not haunted any more, anyway. If it was before, it is not any more," I added hastily.

"Miss Grant, I got an idea," I kept on talking because I did not want to answer any questions about hauntings in case she started going on about it.

"Yes?"

"Let's go back to the cobbler shop and ask Mr. Lane to help us cut the bushes and dig out the hole again, so I can have a short cut, if you and your mother don't mind, that is. It will save steps to the lane by my not having to go way around the block every time."

And then I felt kind of awful about asking to make a short cut through somebody else's garden. It was on a kind of an impulse that I asked, and now felt that I had a lot of nerve to do it. I thought I should apologize right away.

Just then her mother came out, all dressed up, and she said to me, "Hello, dear. It is so nice to have you visit us."

And to Miss Grant, "Don't forget to give her a piece of the nice chocolate cake I baked, Lucille. I am going downtown to do some shopping."

"Yes, Mother."

I was so surprised at how Miss Grant's mother talked to Miss Grant. It was like she was talking to a little girl, so bossy and stern. And Miss Grant was a grown up lady and a school teacher.

Aunt Cora never talked like that to Johnnie and me. She was always loving and kind and never stern even when we were little.

"Do you want your cake now or do we go to Ben's first?" She had waited for her mother to go out the front gate and asked me after the gate clicked.

I gulped, and she got a sparkly look in her eyes as she waited for me to answer. I guessed that her main interest was to see Ben and my short cut was only an excuse.

So I said, "Let's go to the cobbler first."

We ran out of the garden, but walked over to the shop. I guessed that Ben saw us coming because his apron was off and he was standing outside with his hand in his pocket and leaning against the doorpost and the door of the shop was open.

"We came to ask you a favor," Miss Grant called when we got nearer. She sounded bubbly and a little out of breath as if she had been really running, which she hadn't.

"Yes?"

"Thelma dropped in and we got to talking about her house and I mentioned how you and I used to get into the garden when we were children. We tried the loose board again and it came off completely. There is still a small hollow where the hole under the fence was and Thelma wanted to ask you to remove the bushes and dig out the hole again so she can come to visit without going all around the block."

He threw back his head and laughed and laughed. We just stood looking at him because we did not see anything funny about the whole thing.

When he stopped laughing and wiped his eyes with his handkerchief, he said, "There are trespassing laws in effect. Doing what you ask me is breaking and entering private property," and he started to laugh again. "And both of you would be accomplices if we got launched on this career."

So then all three of us got to laughing.

After awhile Ben said, "You should ask your uncle to have a gate made which would give you access into Lucille's garden, if you want to come and go that way—and Lucille's mother has no objections."

I sensed a little sharp edge to his voice at the end.

All of a sudden Lucille stopped laughing and I heard her catch her breath as she turned away. I knew sure as anything right then that there was something shared between them and that Miss Grant's mother was the spoiler.

To break the sudden silence, I said, "Oh, —er— Mr. Lane, do you know my Uncle Eric?"

"Who doesn't?" He shrugged.

"Well, we better be going now, Thelma," Miss Grant said and she took my hand.

Ben put his hand on Miss Grant's arm as she turned away and said, "I'm sorry, Lucille."

She did not say anything as we walked away.

I thought I heard Ben say, "Oh, rats!"

That evening when we were at dinner, I said to Uncle Eric, "There's a school teacher, a Miss Grant, who lives with her mother in a cottage next to our back fence, and I wonder if I could have a gate put in the fence so I could go visit them without going all around the block?"

"I suppose so. Why don't you talk to Olaf about it and he can probably fix something up for you." And to Aunt Cora, "Would that be all right, do you think?"

"If they do not have any objections, I don't."

And then he picked up the thread of his conversation to Aunt Cora and Johnnie. "Well, I wrote to him and asked him for an appointment. His being one of the largest stockholders in the company and having such a big vote in the company, I would like to get to know him. He did not show up at either last year's or this year's stockholder meetings that I know of. But he sure writes a lot of sarcastic letters to the company and there is always very sound business advice in them. I have gone through and studied all the correspondence in his file folders, and even wrote to him several times, suggesting a meeting. There was always a polite refusal and when I dropped into his office on Weybosset Street, he was always away. He must be a very busy man to be away such a lot, and what a coincidence that the largest stockholder should be living in Providence, too."

"Do you have his home address?" Johnnie asked.

"No, only the business phone and the business address are listed in the phone book. And the same information is in the street directory.

"Well, finally, after a couple of years, he wrote me and gave me an appointment at half-past nine in the morning, tomorrow, so you and I, Johnnie, will fare forth to meet this peripatetic and mysterious Mr. Benjamin Lane."

I choked and started coughing and gasping. Aunt Cora jumped up and pounded me on the back and Johnnie ran around the table to hold my arms up over my head and shake them. Finally, I was all right and excused myself to run upstairs.

Oh, my goodness! Mr. Benjamin Lane, the shoe cobbler who was even now probably fixing all our shoes in his cellar, had an office on Weybosset and was the largest stockholder in Uncle Eric's steamship company. Oh, dear, oh, dear! Could there be another Benjamin Lane in Providence? What am I going to do? Of course, I must see Miss Grant right away.

I ran back to get a book, any old book, when I was halfway down the stairs, for an excuse to see Miss Grant in case anybody asked. My intuition told me to get a book and I always did what my intuition told me to, or else I was always sorry.

"Would like anything else to eat, dear?" Aunt Cora asked when I went into the dining room to tell her where I was going. "Are you all right?"

"I'm all right. No, I don't want anything else to eat, thank you, Aunt Cora. I'm going over to Miss Grant's to ask something and I'll be right back to help you."

"It's all right, dear. I'm almost through so don't hurry, but be back soon as it starts getting dark."

"Oh, sure," and I sped away.

There were people sitting on all the stoops of the tenement block and Mr. Guidice, the grocer, in his white apron and straw hat, was standing in the open doorway of his store. As I was shutting the gate of the cottage, I saw the grocer had walked to the side of the store and was watching me.

I pulled the bell knob and heard the bell tinkling inside above the front door. Miss Grant was the first to come around to the front of the house from where she had been in the garden at the back.

I turned to her and whispered, and I don't know why I was whispering, "I must talk to you about Mr. Lane! —something important!"

Just then her mother came around the corner of the house, too. "Oh, hello again," she said.

"Thelma wants to discuss something," and Miss Grant took my book from me and opened it just anywhere.

"I'm going inside. It is starting to get a bit chilly," said the mother. "Don't stay out too long, dear."

So we went to sit on a low bench under the lilac bush over near the front fence and I told Miss Grant all about Ben Lane being a stockholder and having an appointment to see Uncle Eric, who was taking Johnnie with him to Weybosset Street tomorrow.

Miss Grant's eyes got bigger and bigger and then she squeezed my hand so tight that it almost hurt and I had to wriggle it to loosen her grasp.

"Thelma, I must see if that is our Ben. I must! Oh, you dear, dear angel, you will never know what it all means to me!"

"What will you do?"

"I will go in the morning and watch the door on the outside of the building to see if he goes into that door. Do you know the address on Weybosset?"

"No, but Uncle Eric said it was in the phone book."

Miss Grant went inside and got the phone book. We looked under Lane, but there was nothing listed.

"Thelma, do you remember any name that your Uncle or your brother mentioned?"

I shook my head and shut my eyes in order to concentrate very hard. There was a shimmering on the inside of my eyelids and then a barreling spin, and when the spin stopped, I saw letters reading "Benjamin Lane Associates."

I opened my eyes and said, "Let's look under the B's for Benjamin Lane Associates."

And there it was.

"But suppose there's more than one door to the building?" I asked.

"You are right. Well, I will just have to find some vantage point inside the lobby where I will not be noticed."

We sat awhile saying nothing and then I asked, "May I come, too?"

"Well, we may be more conspicuous if there are two of us."

She must have sensed my disappointment, because she added quickly, "You could stand outside somewhere further away but in sight of the door. You could do that."

Chapter 7

There was no echo of a bell when I woke up and I did not hear any sentences. I had to think what was so important about this morning before I remembered about Miss Grant and Ben Lane. I jumped out of bed and dressed real quick.

Everybody was already having breakfast although it was only half-past eight and I asked Aunt Cora if it would be all right for me to do all the beds later on because I wanted to go downtown with Miss Grant.

"Everybody is going downtown this morning!" is all Aunt Cora said.

So I ate real quick and ran over to the cottage. I sat under the lilac bush until Miss Grant came out and she was wearing an old fashioned hat pulled way down over her face and a dark blue raincoat. We let ourselves out through the gate quietly and walked real fast downtown.

I know I stood a long time at the car stop and pretended that I was waiting for my streetcar. I saw Uncle Eric and Johnnie go into the building down the street a ways, but they did not see me. After a few minutes, I saw Mr. Lane across the street and he was walking fast. He turned into the same doorway that Uncle Eric and Johnnie had gone through. Miss Grant was in the lobby and I was hoping that the cobbler wouldn't see her. I was so excited by all this mystery.

It wasn't long when I saw Miss Grant come half running across the street. She grabbed my arm and we both went very quickly before I slowed down after a few blocks.

"Did you see him?" I asked after I caught my breath.

She nodded and she was smiling.

"Did he see you?" I persisted, just wild to know what was going on between the two of them.

"No, he didn't," she said laughing. "There were elevators and there was also a doorway opposite the elevators, off to the side a little, and the door was open a little bit. I think it was an empty store for rent. I slipped in and stood in the dark where I could see the elevator doors. I think I saw your uncle and your brother. It was an older man and a young man who came in together and took the elevator up. And after awhile, I saw Ben come in and get into the elevator."

"So it is the same Benjamin Lane?"

"Oh, yes! Yes! It is!" And she hugged me.

"Well, I'm glad that you're glad, Miss Grant."

"Please call me Lucille. I'm really not that much older than you. I'm only twenty-four."

I gulped. Twenty-four was so very old. But, she did not look old. She looked about as old as one of my new teachers last year, who told the class that she had just graduated from normal school. And she did not act old, either. I supposed that teaching all those little kids in the second grade kept Lucille from getting old.

"All right, Lucille," I said in a small voice. I was almost sixteen, so I was not a kid any more, either. And I would be a senior in high school come September.

Lucille's not being tall, also made her look young, too.

She took my arm and said, "I'm going to let you in on a secret, Thelma, but please do not tell anyone about it."

I almost started putting my arm up to cross my heart but she had hers linked in mine, so I couldn't. "I promise," I said instead.

Golly, I knew more secrets than anyone in the world, I thought. All kinds of secrets with practically everybody I knew. And then I had a lot of secrets of my own that I did not tell anyone, either. I even had a secret with a ghost. Poor Percy. I often wondered where he was now.

"Ben and I were childhood sweethearts," Lucille was saying.

"Really!" I had half guessed it already, but had not been sure.

"Yes, we were. At that time, Benjamin Lane...the street, not Ben... Anyway, there were only three houses on it. Our cottage next to your fence, and there was Ben's house at the end. On the corner where the store is, there was a beautiful Colonial house owned by a very old man and his wife. Where the tenements are, there was an open field. Buttercups, dandelions, and daisies and four-leaf clovers grew all over it. All the land belonged to the people in the corner house.

"Well, Ben is some years older than I am and he watched out for me. He started taking me to school when I went to the first grade. My mother had broken her ankle so she could not take me at that time. And when I got older, Ben used to pick bouquets of flowers for me in the field." She was quiet for a bit, then went on.

"When the old lady in the corner house died, the old man sold the house and the land to Pasco Guidice, and went to live with one of his sons or daughters or grandchildren, I don't really know, but he went to live in Cranston.

"And Mr. Guidice tore out the whole first floor and made it into a grocery store. That beautiful old house was just ruined. Ben's father and my parents were absolutely furious about it. But, it seems that Pasco Guidice had friends in City Hall and nobody could do anything about it.

"Ben had lost his mother when he was quite small. She caught scarlet fever from him when he was sick with it, and he recovered but she died. And his father brought Ben up all by himself. His father would not accept any help from anyone even when my mother offered to help out.

"And then Mr. Guidice started building the tenement block about the time that I was graduating from grammar school. Well, Ben's father, whose name was Benjamin Lane, too—only he was Senior and Ben is Junior—brought suit to stop Guidice from building his tenements because our section of the city is zoned for single-family dwellings. The suit went on for quite awhile and people said that Ben's father lost all his money fighting Guidice. But Guidice succeeded in getting a variance, it seems, and Ben's father lost. My father always said that the suit killed Ben's father because he died even before the tenement block got finished building.

"Well, Ben was going to the state college in Kingston at the time I was going to high school. After he lost his father, Ben left college and boarded up his house, and went away.

"I was so young but I loved him so much, even then. And our families had always sort of felt that we two would marry some day. So Ben told me to wait for him and said that he was going west to make his fortune. I got one post card from him from San Francisco about two years after he was gone. And there were no more cards or letters or anything for years after that."

By this time we were walking very slowly and she was practically talking to herself as if she were way back in the far distance of the past. I got the feeling that I was the first one to whom she was telling all this and that it was the first time that she was talking about something that she had inside for years and years.

"After I finished Normal," she went on, "I substituted for awhile and then got my second grade. And then my father died. He got pneumonia and in three days, he was gone. This left me caring for my mother because Dad's insurance paid only for his funeral. Thank goodness the house was paid for.

"And year before last, Ben showed up all of a sudden and came to ask me to marry him. Well, my mother had a fit. She carried on about his being away so long and never having written, and heaven only knew what he had been up to all the years that he had been away. Of course, I realized that she was worried about herself, too. Who would take care of her? I kept telling her that she must not worry, I would see that she had enough no matter what. But it made no difference. Every time Ben came over, she and he would argue.

"Meanwhile, Ben fixed up the cellar of his house into a shop and City Hall could not stop him because the lane had been zoned so that he could do it. And then he opened up a shoe repair shop and Mother really exploded. She was not going to have her daughter, a school teacher, marrying a cobbler."

I was a little surprised that she was telling me all this private family business, but somehow I seemed to have this effect on people where they always started telling me things. I suppose they knew way deep inside of themselves that I would never repeat anything they told me.

And Lucille went on, "And one day, she and Ben had an awful row and she forbade him to come to our house any more. Well, he stormed out, never to come back."

"Couldn't you explain things to your mother?" I asked.

"I suppose the Commandment of 'Honor thy father and thy mother' was too deeply ingrained. I never opposed my parents and they ruled my life completely. It never even occurred to me to stand up and fight for my happiness," Lucille mused.

"Well, gee whiz, if you love him you can find a way, I bet. And what about your mother maybe marrying somebody again?" the thought had just struck me.

Lucille laughed. "As a matter of fact, Thelma, Pasco Guidice came calling on her with matrimonial intentions about two years after my father died."

"Really!"

"Yes, really!" and she laughed some more. "He dressed up in his Sunday best, but did not wear his straw hat which he wears summer and winter, and brought a five-pound—mind you, a five-pound—box of chocolates, that we ate for a month or so. I was in the kitchen, but saw him get down on his knees and propose to Mother, offering himself and all his worldly possessions. He went on and on about his achievements and how, single-handed, he had made a fortune, denying himself the sweet body of a wife and the noble experiences of fatherhood. He was too old for the latter, he said, but very well endowed for the former."

"So, what happened?"

"Mother gave Mrs. Perrutti a black eye."

"What? And who is, er—, Mrs. Perrutti?"

"Well, first of all, Mother told Guidice that she would think about his proposal for a week or so. Then, the next day, Mrs. Perrutti—she lives in the first doorway next to the store, up on the second floor, and she is a widow—. Well, she came banging on our front door and when Mother opened the door, she stormed in and screamed that Mother was taking Pasco away from her. And she slapped Mother and grabbed at her hair with both hands while she kicked Mother's shins, all the while yelling how she and her Pasco were as good as married and sharing her love.

"Mother swung first one fist into the woman's face and then the other, with all her might. Mrs. Perrutti's head hit the wall and she slid down dazed, into a sitting position. Meanwhile, a whole group of neighbors gathered around our front gate. Mother's hair was all down in disarray, the front door was standing wide open, and here was Mother with the front of her blouse torn, but she paid no attention. She grabbed Mrs. Perrutti under her limp arms from the back, and dragged her out of the hall, down the stoop, along the path to the front gate and out of the gate and dropped her in a heap. One of the woman's shoes had fallen off as Mother was dragging her, and Mother went back to get it and threw that out into the middle of the lane. She dusted her hands off, shut the gate, marched into the house and slammed the door."

"Oh, my goodness!" I had to join Lucille in laughing.

"All of this happened in about a minute. In less time than it takes me to tell about it. I was standing in the middle of the parlor, and before I reacted to go to her aid, she was already dragging her assailant to the gate.

"Her cheek was scratched and there was blood on her lip when she stalked off to the bathroom. I stood rooted to the floor and saw through the parlor curtains, Guidice leading Mrs. Perrutti away. She was leaning on him. She had a black eye that lasted more than a week. And Guidice boasted all over the place how two women fought over his love. I guess all the men in the neighborhood took their hats off to him mentally," and we both laughed again.

"Needless to say," Lucille went on, "he never came back. We never go into his store. He always lifts his hat to Mother and me. I always nod to him, of course, but Mother marches by with her head high. Once in awhile, she says, 'Libertine,' under her breath."

We were at the entrance of Benjamin Lane by now and had stopped.

"Do you think I should tell my aunt and uncle and my brother about Ben?" I asked Lucille.

"I don't know. Really, I don't."

"What are you going to do?"

"I'm going to marry the big lug!" and she laughed so joyously as she skipped down the lane like a little girl. She even did a few dancing steps as she turned to wave to me before she opened her gate. I really liked her for not losing her state of being young inside even though she was so old on the outside.

I did not say anything about Ben to anybody, and did not ask any questions about Uncle Eric's and Johnnie's visit to the Weybosset office in the event that it should slip out that he was the cobbler.

Johnnie did ask me a few days later if I had heard any more of the bell or chime or gong and the words sounding inside of me, so I showed him what I had written, and he got very excited.

He said that he thought maybe Milton wrote his great poetry like that, and that Robert Louis Stevenson wrote like that and he couldn't remember but thought that Arthur Conan Doyle also wrote the Sherlock Holmes stories like that.

After that, I was not scared any more and decided that I was not going crazy, after all. And Johnnie asked me to let him read whatever else I wrote.

A few days afterwards, I woke up in the middle of the night and wrote some more which was a continuation from where I left off the last time. I wrote:

> When the midwife and pastor, assisted by a sleepy Negress, finished their work and the Negress was given the cleanly washed newborn infant to take away, she just stood and stared at it.
>
> The mother was already asleep. Her job was finished and no more was expected of her.
>
> The Negress walked out of the room and was accosted by the small boy who stood with outstretched arms to receive his master. The skinny black little arms encircled that bundle and the gesture was symbolic inasmuch as he stood between his master and the world. He would absorb the shocks and would serve faithfully and gratefully his lord.
>
> The small task of feeding the infant was taken care of by the Negress down in the stinking slave quarters, who gave of her milk whenever Boy appeared with the white baby.
>
> The bathing and clothing of the baby was done by Boy. Somehow, somewhere he learned. No one knew or asked how

or where.

Boy picked out a sunny room up near the top of the house and told—actually told—Mose that he wanted a cradle and all the things needed by the baby for the room. Such a lack of interest on the part of the head of the house in the birth of his son, brought a similar disinterest in the servants. Only Boy was interested, vitally interested. He demanded things for the baby and got them since he was acting for his master. And the black girls were glad to be relieved of new unwanted duties. Thus, the heir of the house of Lane was tossed into the arms of one little black boy who henceforth had a mission in life and "belonged" to someone at last.

Broadly speaking, such an arrangement was not unusual among the wealthy classes of any and all in every century wherein the primary interest is the bodily material self. Ask any very wealthy child if he or she knows the meaning of parental love.

The same state is noted among the very poor where the children are many and provisions scantily supplied.

Thereby is shown the parallelism in the development of character in individuals at the opposite ends of the social scale. In each case the sense of cruelest selfishness is developed to the fullest extent. The wealthy man stoops to crime but buys his way out or has his acts legalized.

The poor man becomes a menace to society and is incarcerated or done away with for the same offenses.

Both of these classes breed vicious individuals in the main. They cannot help themselves since the vibrations are the same in each instance. In one, every whim is catered to, and in the other, every need is disregarded. The circle's ends meet. The personality in each class develops in the same manner. Selfishness becomes paramount.

But, and extremely fortunate is the unfortunate individual to whom it happens, when an outside influence comes in and allows the individual to develop blessed qualities. Such an influence touched Benjamin Lane, Junior, and Boy.

On some of the words, I had to look up the spelling of them later, because I was not sure of them. The story was beginning to be very interesting.

I was just beginning to miss Eda because she did not come around again for a week after I did not go to the library with her the last time. I was wondering what was happening between her and Stephen, when she came over around dinner time and Aunt Cora asked her to stay for dinner. She was so quiet that I asked if she was not feeling well. And she said that she was not sick but she did not feel good, either, because of Stephen. We could not talk much about that at all while we ate dinner, so we helped Aunt Cora very quickly after dinner and went out for a walk.

Of course, we wound up at Benjamin Lane and walked down to where Stephen lived. It was a really hot evening and everybody from the tenements was either sitting on the stoop or had their chairs right out on the sidewalk and were sitting in them. It was a very noisy gathering.

Eda had met Stephen's sister, Mary, one day when Mary came to the library to bring Stephen's lunch after he forgot it. She now called to Eda to come over and join everybody on the stoop. So we went over and Eda introduced her to me. Then Mary introduced us to the people on the stoop and on the sidewalk.

There was the Crespi family which lived on the first floor—the parents and their brood of five children. And on the top floor, there were the Novaks, father and mother, and their grown-up daughter, Wanda, who was about eighteen. She was sitting on the top step and she had a very short dress on and it was cut very low in front and she was twirling a very long string of beads. Stephen was sitting on the bottom step sideways and kept talking to Wanda and they kept laughing. I was wondering where I had seen Wanda before. I was sure that I had seen her somewhere and I remembered her laugh and the way she talked.

Anyway, Stephen only looked once at Eda and said, "Hello," but he did not put his arm around her or anything to show that he liked her.

I could see how miserable she felt, and I got sorry for her and glad at the same time. That was a funny thing how one could feel sorry for somebody and at the same time be glad that it was happening to them. I guessed it was because I felt that she had taken Stephen away from me. I wondered if I should tell her that the only way she could get over her misery was to go somewhere by herself and cry it all out until she felt empty inside. And with that would come the weirdest feeling of being able to see the person who made us suffer, how they really were and what made them be the way they were. It sort of made one wise. And that reminded me of something Aunt Cora said once how everybody could only get wise through suffering. And she said that book learning was O.K. but the school of life was the toughest of all because you never forgot the lessons you learned if it did not do you in. So I supposed that I was sorry about Eda's suffering, but glad that she was getting wise. Still, there was a tiny thought that I was glad, because it was she that came between Stephen and me, like Wanda seemed to be coming between Stephen and Eda right now, and maybe even before tonight. And probably Wanda would suffer some day when some other girl came between her and Stephen.

Just then Stephen leaned over and reached across Eda as she sat on the bottom step between him and me, and put his hand on my knee. He looked at me with half-closed lids and said in his husky voice, "How are you, Thelma? Where have you been keeping yourself? Long time no see!"

It made me laugh in spite of myself because he was trying to act just like a movie hero and practicing to be a lady killer. I picked up his hand and put it back on his knee. I couldn't think of a smart enough answer, so I pretended like I was a movie queen and put my head back and looked at him with half-closed eyes and said in my lowest voice, "I'm O.K., big boy, but if you really wanna know, come up an' see me sometime, an' we'll peel a grape together."

And then Wanda's high voice cut in. "Oh, I know where I met you before, Thelma! I just remembered! You're the girl that Stephen took to his Senior Prom on a dare and won the five dollar bet! I came with my date. Remember me? Wasn't that a scream about the bet?" and she went off into hysterical laughing.

So then everybody started to laugh loudly and making remarks how smart Stephen was to get his prom expenses paid on a bet. And Stephen got a silly and ashamed sort of look on his face. He did not look at me at all when he jumped up and said, "Well, I guess I will go upstairs and help my father down, it must be awful hot up there."

Everybody stopped laughing, of course, because everybody was so sorry about Stephen's father being a cripple.

"Wait a minute," his sister, Mary, jumped up, too. "I will help you."

Mr. Novak got up, too, and all three of them went up to the second floor to help Stephen's father down.

Something inside of my stomach curled up and made a knot.

Mrs. Crespi started telling us how Stephen's mother went to Mass every morning at seven o'clock to pray that her husband would walk again. And once a week, she even lit a votive candle for that intention, after Mass. Mrs. Crespi also said that after seeing Mrs. Seliski light the candle one Sunday, she, too, went up to the altar to light a candle and to pray that Mrs. Seliski's wish would come true.

The knot in my stomach got tighter and I got short of breath. We could all hear noises and talking on the stairs as Stephen's father was being dragged down.

Mrs. Crespi went on to say how Mrs. Seliski worked so hard at taking in other people's washing and that she could hear her scrubbing the clothes on the washboard hours at a time, and ironing even in this hot weather. And everyone agreed that Mrs. Seliski was a real honest to God saint.

Stephen's sister was in Mrs. Crespi's tenement bringing out a chair for her father to sit on, so she did not hear what Mrs. Crespi was saying about her mother.

Mrs. Seliski came down, too, and said that her ironing was finished and how nice and cool it was outside. Stephen's father was sitting with both of his legs stretched out, his back was to the lane, and he was facing the doorway. Quite a few chairs were on the edge of the sidewalk like that, with room for people to pass between the stoop and the chairs along the edge.

Word travelled quickly down the block that Mr. Seliski was outside, and everyone came along to shake his hand and stayed, until practically everyone in the nine families was there. Some of the people had not seen him in over a year or since Christmas or Easter when each of the families was visited by the other eight in turn. Pretty soon Pasco Guidice came along carrying a jug of wine and glasses were gotten from here and there and the wine disappeared very fast. Mr. Crespi brought another gallon from his own cellar and the grocer went to get still another gallon. Someone started singing and then someone remembered how Mrs. Seliski used to play her accordian on summer evenings in years past before her husband's accident and then her husband told her to go get the accordian and they would have a serenade.

Mrs. Seliski protested that she had not played in such a long time and how she had maybe forgotten how the songs went on the accordian, but everyone started begging her so she went upstairs and pretty soon came back with it. Everybody moved around on the stoop until she had enough room to stretch out her arms in playing.

By this time everyone was feeling pretty good from the wine, even the children, who got a little bit in the bottom of their cups because the Italian homemade wine was good for everybody. After my first couple of sips when I wrinkled my face because of the wine being kind of sour and kind of bitter, it started tasting real good.

Mrs. Seliski played fine after she got into the swing of it and people were doing the polka in the middle of the lane and they waltzed and did the quadrille which the Polish people knew how to do and which was a slow and graceful kind of square dancing. And there was lots of singing, of course, in all kinds of languages, even a Jewish song that Mr. Bloomstein from the first floor of the first door, had taught Mrs. Seliski the tune of, a long time ago.

Finally, it started getting late and everyone had to get to bed in order to wake up early if they had to go to work the next morning. So everyone started calling to Mr. Seliski to play the one tune that his wife had taught him and with which he always used to bring to a close the impromptu street concerts, as he walked up and down the whole block and played the tune three times in a row, in years past.

So he held out his arms a little unsteadily to be sure as he sat flushed with the good wine, and when his wife slipped the leather strap over his head and arm — he rose slowly and unsteadily to his feet. The wine that he had drunk made him step out sort of straight legged and he swayed a little, but kept his balance as he started playing the tune and walking down the block.

A sudden silence fell on everyone and they quickly opened a way for him. Everyone's eyes got big and Mrs. Seliski made a sign of the cross in loud Polish on herself and knelt down. The tears were streaming down her face until her face shone under the light of the street lamp. One by one the people were getting down on their knees and Mr. Seliski turned around at the end of the block, first one then another one was calling, "A miracle! A miracle! Mr. Seliski is walking! A miracle!"

I was standing on the edge of the crowd and was nearest to him. I saw a look of fear on his face as he realized that he had been walking and everyone on the block had seen him.

I wondered to myself what he would do now.

Then I saw a sly look on his face, and he started yelling, "I'm walking! Look! I'm walking!" and he was playing and coming back, even shuffling his feet in small unsteady dance steps.

I got hysterical and bolted as fast as I could out of there and ran all the way home to collapse on a bench in our garden across from the statue of the naked lady. First I would laugh until my side ached and then I would cry. I was shaking and could not stop laughing or crying.

Then I saw Johnnie come running out of the gazebo and he grabbed me and shook and slapped my cheek, not too hard but enough to stop my wild laughing and crying. He sat on the bench and held me tight until I stopped shaking. He kept sort of crooning, "There, there, Bunny, it's all right. Don't worry. Everything is all right. There, there—"

"Oh, my gosh!" I said after I finally stopped shaking, and I told Johnnie everything. Just everything about how I got a crush on Stephen and saw his father exercising on the roof (only Johnnie thought I saw it from Mom and Dad's room window up in the attic, instead of my hideaway's window)— and how Eda got a crush on Stephen, too. And how Eda and I went walking in the lane, and the party and the wine and the music and dancing and singing. Then I told how Mrs. Crespi told us all about Mrs. Seliski's praying for a miracle and lighting candles in church. Then, how Mr. Seliski got drunk and forgot that he was not supposed to walk, but got up and went stiff-legged and swaying up the lane—

Well, then Johnnie started laughing and I got to laughing again, too. We were both hanging on to each other and laughing to beat the band. We'd stop, then look at each other in the bright moonlight and start laughing again. I really got weak from all that laughing.

Johnnie then told me that he was glad of my coming along when he was sitting in the gazebo and feeling kind of sad because he was saying goodbye to the house for awhile and was all packed to go away to San Francisco and be on the ship with Captain Olafsen.

I felt a little pang that Johnnie would be going away and hugged him tight and told him I would miss him. He thought that maybe he would be home for Thanksgiving but was coming back for Christmas for sure. And he said that he would write a lot and tell me all his new adventures.

We were quiet for a bit and did not say anything. Finally, Johnnie turned to me and asked if I had heard any more of the chime and written more on my dictation. So I told him that I wrote some more and we went inside and he read what I wrote.

When he finished, he looked at me in a very peculiar way.

Then, he said, "Bunny, you are a special kind of person. I am beginning to believe that you are a catalyst of some sort."

I did not know what he meant, but did not say anything.

"Somehow, in some way, you make things change for people when they come in contact with you. It is always a drastic change, but a change for the better. If there is something wrong in people's lives, things rearrange themselves and things come right.

"Look at this thing tonight and that man who had been vampirizing his family for years. I wonder if everything would have happened as it did, if you had not gone there tonight. But, you went and showed up Stephen for the flirt he is, and to cover his confusion and get sympathy again established on his side, he brought his supposedly lame father into the picture, and the rest is history."

I was listening to him real close.

"Well, look at Aunt Cora and Uncle Eric," Johnnie continued. "It was because of wanting to adopt you that they got married. They were crazy about each other, too. But, I wonder if they would have had the nerve to get married if you had not been around to provide the excuse."

And then I thought of other things that had happened, but which scared me. I thought of how Mom and Dad got killed. I wondered if it was because they did not go to Johnnie's high school graduation, but went to a Depression Party instead.

Then, I thought of how Percy got me so mad, and then he vanished.

But, I never got hurt by Clifford, only I did not return his love, so why did he have to die? I liked him a lot, too, and felt sorry for him.

"So, my dear Bunny," Johnnie was saying, "I have thought of your unusual self more than once, and I must admit defeat in trying to figure out the kind of person you are. Whatever it is, you are unconscious of it."

If I felt a little afraid, I also was a little sad as I fell asleep after I went to bed. I, too, could not figure out what kind of a person I was.

❖❖❖

Chapter 8

There was a lot of dictation on this particular morning and I had gotten used to it, so wrote very fast:

Boy held the baby gingerly and changed his swaddling clothes after bathing the cooing infant.

Meanwhile, somewhere around the time of the baby's arrival in the Lane home, the news came via Mose that the only book now obtainable at the stationers was the Bible. Such was the abundance of seditious literature that it was sold openly in all stationers' shops. Then, the order came to cease publication and distribution of these printings on the pain of fines and imprisonment.

Since Lane, Senior, had an extensive library, he resolved immediately to go over his collection and hide anything savoring of freedom for the colonies. He knew that the order to the stationers would be followed by a systematic search of private premises when least expected, sooner or later.

Whatever else the senior Lane was, he was no fool. Sometime during his son's first days on this earth, the father cleared out the library of suspect literature and hid the items well. This precaution served a double purpose. It saved the books and pamphlets for the time being and eventually served as a source of inspiration to the younger Lane when the proper time came.

To go back, sometime during the first night of the baby's birth, the grandmother hobbled out of the hole of a room where she lived up in the attic, to investigate the bustle which was going on under her room.

This old woman was to be the guiding factor in Boy's bringing up of the infant. Boy's proclivities for getting the most out of any given situation, managed to instill enough life and interest in the old woman's half-dead body to revive her into being a meddling, querulous but highly efficient old scold. Thus, she became the guiding light to Boy in the matter of rearing little Ben.

After the old woman realized the utter indifference of the parents to their child, the awakened awareness of the situation jolted her out of the dream world into which she had retreated. In fact, she could and would bring support to the fore if Boy's activities clashed with anybody else's.

In such manner all the honors of the battlefield were carried off by the aristocratic old dame and the little colored child who was seldom seen without the white baby in his arms.

Activities in the house resumed their natural course with the passing of time. The mother of the baby again received guests after two weeks, and accorded them a graphic description of her suffering. The females of her circle, whose only function was to conceive and bear children, delegated the rest of the agony and anxiety of bringing up a human being to the servants.

All the females who came to call on Elvira, clucked in sympathy as their own recollections swam to the surface of their consciousness.

The father, beyond a glimpse of the red puckered face, did not set eyes on his son until many months later when he stumbled over the baby as the tot was crawling under the watchful eyes of Boy, about the stable yard.

"Who is that?" he roared at Boy, who was not a bit frightened.

"Don't you know your own son?!" a shrill and angry, cracked old voice swirled around his ears and a cane lashed smartly at his silk clad calves. He jumped and whirled to confront his old mother whose screaming voice had not abated as she flung a string of vituperation at him which would have shamed a seasoned tramp.

He fled, his calves quivering from the pain of the beating his mother had administered.

The frail, but spry old dame was feared and loved by the servants. They sprang to do her bidding, yet they loved her. Thus, once again she assumed charge of the house where it touched her own, Boy's, and the baby's lives.

Perhaps it was a good thing that she did not assume the responsibility of running the whole house because that would certainly have brought consequences of no mean order between her and her daughter-in-law.

And there was no more, though I waited for a good while but the story did not resume. The only reason that I could think of for hearing the story, was that I got very interested in why the name of a man was the name of a street in back of our house, and wondered who the man was that gave his name to the street. In some mysterious way I tuned into the story of Benjamin Lane, but I could not say that I liked him. He kept slaves and he certainly did not live in Providence. So where did he live? And what connection could there be between the Benjamin of the story and the street in back of our house? And in some way it tied in with the Benjamin Lane that was the cobbler only he was more than a cobbler.

I supposed that I would eventually find out if the dictation kept up.

And then a thought came to me which was so enormous that I almost fainted. The thought came that maybe I could tune in like a radio to any past time in history and find out what really happened, and if I could tune in on the past, then maybe I could tune in on the future?

The thought scared me so much that I got dressed in a hurry and ran down to be with Aunt Cora because I could not stand being alone with myself.

Johnnie was all dressed and there were a couple of suitcases standing near the front door which I saw as I went into the dining room and sat down to breakfast.

Aunt Cora was saying, "It is good that you are all dressed, Bunny. I was going to come up to wake you. Johnnie will be leaving in another half hour and we will drive him to the Union Station."

"Are you going, too, Uncle Eric?" I asked.

"Only as far as New York, where Johnnie changes to another train."

"Are you excited about going, Johnnie?" I asked him.

"Oh, sure! Who wouldn't be?"

Then Uncle Eric said to Johnnie, "As soon as we get to New York I will send a telegram to Captain Olafsen at what time you will be arriving after your change in Chicago, assuming that the trains will be on schedule. Should there be a delay in Chicago, you may want to send him another telegram. Also, I will ask the captain to make you a reservation at the St. Francis Hotel in San Francisco."

"How long will I be staying at the hotel?"

"It will be a permanent reservation where you will stay between trips with Captain Olafsen until you familiarize yourself with the lumber transport business, and then you will be at our offices every day in San Francisco after you stop shipping out."

"I'm looking forward to going, Uncle Eric. And I cannot tell you what it means to me to fall into a job right out of college when so many thousands of others are hunting for something to do."

"The feeling is mutual, my boy. I am glad to have someone with your capabilities to gradually work your way into running the business. If truth must out, my first and only choice of professions is teaching."

Then we got into Uncle Eric's old Ford, which Olaf the captain's son was driving, and went to the station. And Aunt Cora cried a little when she kissed and hugged Johnnie. Of course, I kissed and hugged him, too, but I did not feel sad although I knew that I would miss him.

Eda was sitting at our front door when we got back. "Where did you all go? I was waiting a long time."

"We went to Union Station to see Johnnie off to San Francisco. And Uncle Eric went with him as far as New York."

"Well, gee whiz! You could of let me know that he was going this morning, and I could of come by to say so-long."

I could not resist being a little mean and said, "I thought that you did not care about Johnnie any more."

"Oh, you!" and she shoved me.

I thought of something and said to Aunt Cora, "What about all those shoes being mended for Uncle Eric and Johnnie and us? I think they are done by now."

"Are they? Well, I will give you the money and you can get them if you will. We will put Johnnie's shoes into his closet for when he comes home. He had enough shoes to take with him."

Eda did not want to go to the cobbler's with me and I did not mention Stephen to her. I knew she would tell me all about it when she got good and ready.

So I said, "Well, I have to go to the cobbler, and what are you going to do?"

"Oh, I guess I'll mope around awhile at my grandmother's and then go to the Majestic. There's a new picture starting today—a musical. Wanno go?"

"N-no, not particularly."

All of a sudden, I thought of my real father. So I asked Eda, "Are you going to get any movie magazines?"

"Oh, sure."

"Let me have them after you finish?"

"Sure. I may want to cut out some pictures though."

"That's O.K. But let me see them before you cut them out."

"All right. Well, so-long."

"So-long."

And I went to Benjamin Lane after Aunt Cora gave me some money.

Boy, am I dumb! I thought to myself as I was walking along the lane. The man I am writing about must be an honest-to-God ancestor of the cobbler who is not really a cobbler, but maybe does it as a hobby because he has a business office already. I wondered if I ought to show him what I had written and decided to wait.

When I went down into the shoe repair shop, I saw Lucille sitting on a high stool at the bench and I sensed a sharp tingle in the air as if they were having a fight or something. Both of them turned to look at me as I came in.

"Hello, Lucille," I said. "Good morning, Mr. Lane. I came to get the shoes."

"Hello, Thelma," Lucille said and went on from where I interrupted her, I suppose.

"But, you must talk to her. She is my mother, and she is going to be your mother-in-law."

I must have made some sort of a sound because they both looked at me again.

Lucille laughed and hopped off the stool to come and stand near me. "As you see," she said to me, "I have finally said, 'Yes' to Ben's proposal. I would also like to have you as my maid-of-honor."

"Me?" I could hardly believe my ears.

"Yes, you!" and she laughed. "You are sort of responsible for bringing Ben and me together, if you will remember. You came asking about the history of Benjamin Lane, the street—and I brought you here to meet Benjamin Lane, the man. Remember?"

I nodded.

"Ben and I have not been talking for a few years."

"Well, young lady," Ben broke in and said to Lucille, "it was entirely your own fault. I waited patiently for your answer, you must admit."

"Why didn't you come to get it?"

I could see that as far as they were concerned, I was not there any more for all the attention they paid to me. So I sat down on the lowest stair at the door and waited for them to finish fighting.

"Why didn't I come to get the answer, she asks me! Didn't your mother as much as throw me out of the house? And what's more, she told me that she didn't care if I never came back. Didn't even give me a chance to tell the reason that I did not write. I was on ships sailing all over creation trying to make a living and keep up on the taxes on this old house. How could I write when I did not have enough to offer? Sure, I opened up a shoe repair shop. I did not want to be idle. I learned to be a cobbler while I was at sea. In fact, I am the best one around. I came when I knew I could support a wife. But your mother flatly refused a cobbler for a son-in-law. Now, say it is not so?"

"Did you propose to my mother or to me?"

"I had to ask somebody for your hand in marriage, and your father is dead."

"Oh, my Lord! I happen to be free, white, and over twenty-one!

Can't you get that through your thick head? I do not need anyone's permission to marry. I can marry anyone I want and nobody can stop me."

They were shouting at each other and I thought that it was a funny way for two people in love to decide to get married. I propped my elbows on my knees, put my chin into my cupped hands and looked first at one then at the other, back and forth as they yelled at each other.

He got a sly look on his face. "So now you're ready to marry a cobbler?"

"When I love a man, I'd marry him if he were a ditch digger."

"You will have to give up teaching."

"I know."

"Who will support your mother?"

"I will."

"How?"

"I'll — I'll take in washing!"

He laughed.

"Oh, shut up, Ben Lane. You know I can be on the substitute list and make enough each month to pay for her needs."

"But suppose you get a little one?"

"Ben! You asked me to marry you, and stomped out of the house before I gave you my answer. It wasn't my fault that you took it on yourself to ask my mother if I could marry you. That was a dumb thing to do and a very stupid one, at that. The Victorian Age is long gone. Women even have the vote."

"Well, how was I supposed to know? I never had any sisters!"

"Oh, Lord save me! Don't interrupt! I waited and waited and waited for you to come and get your answer to your proposal. But when I saw that you were too immature to stop sulking, I came myself. It may be a trite saying, but oh! how true it is, that every woman must keep a school because every man is born a fool. And now you parade me all those objections, so I have no alternative but to withdraw my affirmative answer as well as my person from your vicinity. Let it not be said that I have an unfinished chapter in my life," and she reached up to snap her fingers under his nose.

He wrapped his arms around her, picked her up and sat her on the bench among the shoes. Then he reached under his apron into his pocket and pulled a little box out.

"Before you go sky-tailing off, I have something of yours that I have been carrying for many years, and I have no use for it, so you may as well have it."

He snapped the box open and took out a ring which he put on Lucille's finger. The light caught it and there was a brilliant flash. I sat with my mouth open. I used to see big diamonds in Tilden & Thurber's window, but this one was even bigger than the one Uncle Eric gave to Aunt Cora.

Lucille gasped and stared with her mouth open, too. All she could do was look at it. Ben put his hand under her chin and bent his head down to kiss her. Very slowly she put her arms around his neck and they kissed a long time.

I sighed. It was so beautiful, like a movie just before THE END.

I could have cried I was so happy for them. I must have made some sort of noise when I stood up, because Ben looked in my direction.

"Oh, your shoes are ready," he said and I waited.

He dropped all of them into a paper bag and handed it to me without telling me how much I owed on them, and turning to Lucille, he said, "And I am not going to go into your house to tell your mother that I am going to marry you." And he stuck his lip out.

"Coward!" But Lucille was half-smiling.

"The biggest one you ever saw where she is concerned. She is a real battle-ax!"

"Don't worry, she'll melt when she sees this rock."

"There's more where that came from."

"Yeah? Ben, why are you being a cobbler?"

"A few reasons. Keep predatory females off my back— Keep track of you— Spy on you— And beat up any guys who came after you."

"You're nuts!"

"Sure am to have waited for a spitfire like you. I'll bet you turn out just like your mother."

"Well, you just bet I will have to, in order to keep any predatory females from getting you away from me."

And they both started kissing again, so I scooped up the bag and left. I was wondering what Ben would have said and how he would have acted if he knew that Lucille and I already knew about his being more than just a cobbler. Well, he was never going to find out from me and that's for sure. And maybe Lucille would tell him some day when they are both very old.

I decided not to tell Aunt Cora yet that I was going to be a maid-of-honor to somebody that she had never met and whom I met only a short while ago. Funny thing, I felt as if we all had known each other for a very long time and as if we had been away from each other and have come back together again. It seemed like the most natural thing in the world.

When I walked in the kitchen door, Aunt Cora was rolling out some pie dough and there were sliced apples already to put in the filling. Off in back of the house, I could hear sawing and hammering and guessed that Olaf was making a gate between Lucille's garden and ours.

"Would you like me to put the mended shoes away?" I asked Aunt Cora. And I put the money she gave me to pay for them on the table.

"Just put them inside the bedroom doors, dear."

When I came down again, I thought for the hundredth time what a funny rich family we are with Aunt Cora doing all the cooking and everybody else helping with the house work. Even Uncle Eric washed windows and he and Johnnie scrubbed and waxed the floors and beat the carpets. The only help Aunt Cora had was a washerwoman who washed and ironed our clothes and things. Anyway, we all made such fun with the work in the house, that it did not seem like work at all.

Aunt Cora was putting the pies in the oven when I came into the kitchen.

"How much did the cobbler charge for the shoes?" she asked.

"Nothing. He just put them in the bag and gave them to me without wanting the money I held out to him."

"Why did he do that?"

"I don't know. Maybe because he was busy getting engaged to Lucille."

"Who's Lucille?"

"That's Miss Grant."

"Do you know her?"

I was being very patient because I had already told Aunt Cora about Lucille Grant.

"She's the teacher that lives in back of our house and Olaf is making a gate between our two gardens."

"Oh, yes! I see! That's right. Now I remember. And she got engaged to the cobbler?" Aunt Cora peered at me real hard.

I nodded.

"How peculiar. One would think she would want to marry a little better than a cobbler."

"Well, he's a cobbler, but he really isn't a cobbler," I flew to Lucille's defense. And by this time I was wishing that I had not come back to the kitchen.

"What do you mean, he isn't a cobbler, Bunny? Either he is or he isn't, so which is it?"

Oh, dear, I thought to myself. Now I was really flopping around. Well, if I have to tell, I will. Aunt Cora was sitting on a tall stool and waiting for me to answer.

"Well— er— mm— Do you remember how Johnnie and Uncle Eric went to see Mr. Lane at his office on Weybosset?"

"Yes."

"Well, that's the cobbler."

"What?"

I could see that Aunt Cora found this hard to believe. I was totally miserable by now and feeling like I had betrayed some very good friends.

"Well, it is sort of a hobby," I went on slowly. "Mr. Lane learned to do it when he was sailing on ships, and— er— now he does it— but not much— I think." By now I had run out of words.

"You don't say!" Aunt Cora hopped off the stool and put the money in her pocketbook. "You do know the right people. I must say."

I had a feeling that this was not complimentary to Eda, somehow.

After awhile, she asked again, "And how did you meet Mr. Lane?"

"Lucille introduced me."

"Mmmmmm—"

I jumped up and ran out into the garden after I said a quick, "Excuse me, Aunt Cora."

I did not want her to ask me any more questions. How little I knew that it was only the beginning of a long and complicated thing later on.

As usual, I headed for the gazebo, which I always did when I wanted to sit and think. And that is where Eda found me. I really felt sorry for her. She looked as if she had not slept all night, and her eyes were sort of red, so I guessed that maybe she had been crying. I did not say anything and neither did she. She just kept sighing and fidgeting.

After awhile, I couldn't stand it any more, so I asked, "Did you go to the Majestic?"

She shook her head from side to side.

So I said, "Maybe you want we should go to the library?" I thought that she might want to see Stephen.

"No, I was there already," and she flung her arms around me and cried and cried and cried, very noisily and very wetly. But, I didn't care that she was making my dress all wet, even though it was the kind of material that showed where the wet part was. I just patted her back and let her cry it all out. And all the while I was remembering how I cried myself to sleep over Stephen, too. But, all the pain and disappointment were gone now. I wondered if it was the fate of every girl to cry over boys and figured it must be.

"He didn't even look at me," Eda wailed. "He was hanging around and making eyes at one of the clerks at the circulation desk."

I made some sort of comforting noises and she blew her nose and wiped her eyes. She was hiccupping from crying so hard.

"You don't know the half of it, Thelma. I went over to him to say, 'Hello, Stephen,' and he just looked right through me as if I wasn't there."

"Don't feel bad, Eda. He's just a big old flirt, that's what he is, and not worth crying over."

"And the way he held my hand and looked into my eyes and bent me back like Rudolph Valentino, and kissed me real slow and passionate like. Oh, Thelma!" and she dissolved into tears once more.

"Well, you better forget all about him," I advised her coldly.

"Ooh! I'm going to get even with him! You just wait and see, Thelma! Some way, I'm going to get even with him," she was looking very fierce as she said it.

"I wouldn't waste my time if I were you."

"Well, he can't fool around with me."

"What are you going to do?"

"I don't know yet. But you just wait."

Well, at least Eda was over being sad and was more natural in being mad.

I thought the pies should be ready by now and we went in to lunch. Something nice to eat is always good for a broken heart.

When Olaf came in for lunch, he said that he had cleared out a space between the back gate in the iron fence, which we did not know that we even had one there, and the wooden fence on the outside at Benjamin Lane. He said that he was making a gate in the wooden fence. Also, he said that it took a lot of filing and oil to make the iron fence gate work again because the hinges and latch were so rusted, even though they had been painted over many times. It looked to him like the gate had not been used for a very long time.

So, after lunch, we all went to see how he was making the gate. And Lucille's mother was already there, so I introduced Aunt Cora to her.

"I am delighted to meet you at long last!" said Mrs. Grant. She was being so smiling and effusive. "Of course, I knew who my neighbors across the back fence were, but the opportunity never presented itself."

So she and Aunt Cora laughed a little, and then Aunt Cora said, "As you see, we are still repairing and fixing up and painting— It is such a long process, since the house had been vacant for such a long time. And being so busy, one does not have much time to even look around the neighborhood."

I marvelled at how well Aunt Cora spoke after studying good English all by herself. And I marvelled at how Aunt Cora was pleased to meet Mrs. Grant now that she knew that her daughter was going to marry a rich man. And I marvelled at Mrs. Grant not minding a gate into her back garden, because we were rich. And then I marvelled that I had such thoughts of their being snobbish, and wondered if I were the biggest snob of them all, but I didn't think so. I was quickly through marvelling because Aunt Cora then said, "I have just heard the wonderful news about your daughter."

I wanted to run and hide. Mrs. Grant got such a surprised look on her face, and stood with her mouth a little open. We all heard her front gate click and she turned away from us. Pretty soon her back door opened and Lucille came out, followed by Ben Lane.

The thought flashed through my mind that Lucille had finally persuaded Ben to come back and face her mother.

We heard Mrs. Grant gasp, sort of, and she put her hand to her face. Lucille came half-running and held out her left hand to her mother. The diamond flashed in the noon sun like a beacon.

"Ben and I got engaged, Mother."

I sensed right away that she was glad we were all there and that her mother was not all by herself at this important time.

Aunt Cora called out, "Well, how wonderful!" And she came right into the garden and took Lucille's hand to take a closer look at the ring. "How beautiful! Simply gorgeous!"

And she turned to Ben and shook his hand. "Congratulations, young man!" even as I was busily introducing him to her.

She kept on talking. "Oh, I have heard a lot about you from my husband and nephew! Yes, indeed! Your valuable suggestions regarding my husband's business are very much appreciated, you may be sure."

All this was going on while we were standing around and Mrs. Grant was blinking and swallowing as if things were happening too quickly.

Once again I marvelled at how Aunt Cora got hold of the situation. In no time at all she made all the connections in her mind without thinking it over that Mr. Benjamin Lane was the same person that Uncle Eric and Johnnie went to see, that he was now engaged to Lucille, and that he was the cobbler. It had taken a long time, specially, for her to get Lucille and her mother being our neighbors, straightened out.

Nobody was still saying anything, and Aunt Cora went on, "What an interesting hobby, you have, Mr. Lane. Fixing shoes! My niece tells me you picked it up while at sea. I must say that you did a very fine job on the ones my niece brought back. And I do thank you for refusing payment! Let me assure you that we will not take advantage and will be very careful not to abuse the privilege of your mending our shoes!" and she patted his hand before letting it go.

It was amazing how Aunt Cora told it all. Neither Lucille nor Ben had to open their mouths to do any explaining. So Mrs. Grant put her arms around Lucille and started to laugh and cry at the same time. And Ben put his arms around them both.

Aunt Cora called to Eda and me and Olaf, "Come children! We must get back to the house."

"Oh, Thelma! Did you see that ring!" Eda whispered fiercely into my ear.

I nodded.

"Boy! When I get engaged, I want a diamond like that!" Eda seemed to be forgetting about Stephen.

Chapter 9

It was toward the middle of July that I heard the chime waking me up and wrote some more:

> As it was, the rule of drinking, party giving and gambling went on unchanged. The mistress of the house spent her days with seamstresses, milliners, or went calling. The rest of the time, she spent in planning parties to give, or planning what to wear when she went to parties.
>
> The Lane household was essentially no different from a great deal of wealthy family households. Everything was done with one end in view—personal pleasure. Sometimes vague stirrings of conscience diminished pleasures momentarily. Elvira remembered that she had a child. But the remembrance was hastily thrust back into its little box in her mind and the lid tightly shut on it. Barely was the persistently annoying fact forgotten, when it popped up again in full bloom to spoil the moment.
>
> The ladies who came to call on the mistress of the Lane estates were no better than she. They moaned and groaned about their hardships and did nothing more strenuous than propel their befrocked, beribboned, and becurled selves on the round of their neighbors and exerted themselves lifting cups of tea. Ah, the rigors of daily living was sometimes more than they could stand. Only the thought of other ladies dressing more beautifully and giving more spectacular balls, kept their poor, overfed, overdressed, overpampered selves going at all. Really, life was too exhausting.
>
> Benjamin Lane, Senior, knew he had a son, of course, but the mere idea of doing something or even taking an interest in his son's upbringing filled him with an uneasy reluctance.
>
> Women's affair! He dismissed it summarily.
>
> In that manner, the sole response to the necessary needs in taking care of the infant was made by a very inexperienced but willing little black boy and by an experienced, roused to sense of duty, dirty and bad-smelling old woman.
>
> The child thrived between these two. It had its fill of clean fresh air which was denied the more carefully brought up scions of wealthy estates. It rolled naked in the sunshine because Boy would have liked to have had the little white baby of a darker hue. It ate greens and vegetables, milk and eggs, and other things which made it well and strong with sound bones and good flesh. He was being brought up right while pampered, puling, infants and growing youngsters

languished on pastries and delicacies of all sorts.

Many days, the mothers of these children spent alone in darkened rooms with their imaginary ills. They emerged, wearing suffering miens which evaporated when they forgot to act. Such a one was Mistress Benjamin Lane.

Days and nights were hot, but our house was cool, 'specially downstairs and out in the garden under the trees.

I went to stay at Eda's grandmother's summer cottage on Rocky Point for a week, but it was not so much fun any more as it used to be. Maybe it was because I was growing up. And Eda got very friendly with a new family that had a boy about our age, so when Uncle Eric came up to see if everything was all right, I went back home with him. I could see that Eda was kind of relieved to see me go, because the boy used to look at me more than he looked at her. She made some remarks about wishing I could stay a little longer, but I could see that she was wishing I would hurry up and leave.

I caught Uncle Eric looking first at me and then at her, back and forth a few times, then he shook his head as if he did not understand something as he put my suitcases in the rumble seat of Johnnie's roadster which he was driving while Johnnie was away.

I felt that I should explain something to Uncle Eric. So I said, "When we were very poor, Uncle Eric, and lived in the poor section on the other side of the avenue, nobody wanted to play with me. But, Eda always came to play with me. Even her mother told her not to come on our street, and she said she would give Eda a licking if she caught her coming over to our house. But Eda came anyway even though she could stay only a little bit and had to run home before her mother came home from work."

"I did not know that," Uncle Eric said.

"It was only after Aunt Cora bought our house that Eda's mother let her come over. So when she is not real nice a lot of times, and takes a lot of advantage of me, I remind myself of the time when she was the only one who wanted to be my friend."

"That explains a lot of things, Bunny. Yes, it explains and confirms a lot about you and what a dear, thoughtful, and wise young lady you are."

It made me feel so good to hear him say that. I leaned over and hugged his arm, and he patted mine.

After awhile, as we were driving, he asked, "And how is your friend, the teacher, these days? Lucille, I think."

"Oh, she is very excited about getting married and not having to go back to work and everything. And she is fixing up Ben's house for them to live in."

"When are they planning to get married?"

"In October, because it will take that long to fix up their house. Isn't it funny how their house and our house used to be all shut up and everything not used for a long time?"

"Indeed?"

"Oh, yes! After Ben stopped working on ships, he came back and only fixed up the cellar to be his shop and just used the side door opening on the lane. And he lived in back of the shop."

"I see."

"Do you know, Uncle Eric, that Ben's house is even older than ours?"

"Is it?"

"Oh, yes! It used to be an inn way back in Colonial times."

"You don't say!"

"And one of the rooms upstairs, way in back, used to be a meeting room of some kind with benches on two sides and a raised platform in the middle, which is like a triangle. And then, at the far wall, there is another platform with three steps going up to it."

Uncle Eric was listening very hard.

"And Ben says that Lucille can fix up the rest of the house, but that room they will leave as it is. He says that it must have been used in Colonial times and maybe it is very historical."

"I dare say."

"And they are going to shut up the cobbler shop for good and they will start using their front door again which opens onto the avenue— where they have an iron fence that looks something like ours."

"Perhaps the same ironmonger put up their fence and ours," was Uncle Eric's comment.

"Must be. Anyway, Uncle Eric, it is all very exciting. And Mrs. Grant is making Lucille's wedding dress and my maid-of-honor's dress—" I clapped my hand over my mouth because I had not told anybody yet that I was going to be the maid-of-honor.

By this time we were inside our driveway and Uncle Eric drove the roadster into the carriage house and stopped.

"So! You are going to be the maid-of-honor at Mr. Lane's marriage!" He slapped his knee and laughed and laughed until he had to wipe his eyes.

I was glad that he did not get mad or anything like that.

He was still chuckling when we came into the house and the first thing he said to Aunt Cora, who met us at the door, was, "What do you say, my love, to the fact that our Bunny was asked to be maid-of-honor at Benjamin Lane's marriage?"

"Oh, Bunny! Really?" and she hugged me.

Whew! That was such a relief that they were not scolding me for not telling them before.

"What will you be wearing, dear? When is the wedding? Where will they get married? Oh, dear, we must talk to the bride right away!" Aunt Cora was fluttering around like a mother bird.

"Well— er— Lucille's mother is making the dresses for the wedding—," I began.

"How nice! Let us have lunch right away and go pay Mrs. Grant a call to enquire about the arrangements," and she hurried us into the dining room.

I was feeling so nervous and expecting any minute to be asked why I did not mention any of it before. And I did not know why I did not talk about it before.

The worst of it was that both Lucille and her mother somehow got the idea that I had already told at home about the wedding plans. I don't know where they got the idea. Mrs. Grant felt that it was such a great honor my being the maid-of-honor and having the Professor and Mrs. Hawkins, as she called Aunt Cora and Uncle Eric, be the guests at her daughter's wedding. And I did not even know that my aunt and uncle would come to the wedding because they were always doing something important or going somewhere important. Things were just happening too fast for me to cope with.

As it turned out, I need not have worried at all because Aunt Cora took charge right away. After lunch she and I went over to Lucille's through the back gate that Olaf made and took away the bridesmaids' material that Lucille had already bought. Lucille was having two bridesmaids besides me, and Aunt Cora sewed all three dresses. I think Aunt Cora was more excited about the wedding than I was. She was running back and forth through the back gate between the Grant's house and ours all the time. She was better at fitting than Mrs. Grant and even helped her with Lucille's dress. Our house got very busy with the bridesmaids coming practically every day to get fitted and staying for dinner. I had not seen Aunt Cora so busily happy in quite awhile.

And when the dresses for us attendants and Lucille's dress were all done, Aunt Cora and Mrs. Grant made dresses for themselves. And then they got busy with the reception and what they would do and what food would be served and all the rest of the things that go with getting married.

Ben wanted the wedding reception to be held at his house in the big living room that used to be the old inn's main room downstairs. And the wedding was going to be at Grace Church, so everything was set on Lucille's side.

Sometime during all the goings on, Ben found out that Uncle Eric was Aunt Cora's husband. With Ben being such a private sort of person and not having any close friends, he got Uncle Eric to be his best man one evening when Lucille and her mother and he came over to talk about the wedding plans.

And then it came out how Ben got to be the largest stockholder in Uncle Eric's steamship company, and why he wrote those hateful letters about how badly the company was being run. So, Uncle Eric immediately made him President of the company, while he, himself, became Chairman of the Board.

It was through Uncle Eric's old uncle that Ben made his fortune. Ben always thought that he would inherit the whole steamship company some day because he did not know that the old man had a nephew. It was such a blow to him after working so hard and building up the business, when the old man, practically on his death bed, fired him and gave him two million dollars and more than a third of the shares of stock in the company. Ben felt so awful because it was really he that built up the business where it was so successful.

Uncle Eric and Ben figured out that the old man had removed everything from the files that referred to Ben. Uncle Eric never found anything about Ben except that he had the shares of stock. So it was no wonder that Ben was so resentful about what was happening to the company with Uncle Eric knowing nothing about running it. Captain Olafsen was the only one that kept the company going, but he did not know much about the business end of it.

Anyway, everything was straightened out and everybody was happy once more. And once more everybody got back to the wedding plans.

When it came to making up a list of wedding guests, Ben had only the people in his office downtown to invite – the secretary and her family, also the accountant and his family, and the file clerk and her family.

But Lucille and her mother knew so many friends that their side of the church was going to be all filled.

Ben asked Uncle Eric to write to Johnnie about the wedding and

Johnnie wrote back that he would make a quick trip in October in time for the wedding, so that was one more on Ben's side of the church.

And then, Ben invited all the families on the lane to come to his wedding seeing as he had been mending all their shoes for as long as he had the shop and they all knew him. Aunt Cora and Uncle Eric were wondering if they would come to the Protestant church seeing as they were mostly all Catholic, except the Bloomsteins who were Jewish, and the Franklins who were Baptists. Of course, Eda and her grandmother got asked and they, too, were Catholic. In the end, half the Protestant church was filled with Catholics and one Jewish family.

It made me wonder at how things work out sometimes. I was remembering how Ben's father fought and fought to keep all those families out of the lane. And then, all those families got invited to come to his son's wedding. It was almost as if there is a very great plan at work, greater than all the people put together, which gets done no matter who wants to stop it.

All those families had to come to live on Benjamin Lane, like Aunt Cora had to buy our house, and now all our lives were getting mixed up somehow. The wonder of it all was that we were all so different in every way. We had different religions, we came from different nationalities, our lives were lived differently, yet there had to be some sort of a tie that made it possible for us to understand one another, and it had to be more than all of us being able to talk in English. All I could think of was that we were all human beings.

It was the beginning of August when I heard the echo of the chime again and wrote:

> The early infancy of Benjamin Lane, Junior, progressed normally as could be expected under these circumstances. Boy wore down resistance which may have existed on Mose's part and had the run of the house, but did not show himself to the master and mistress of the house. Some vague fear that his charge might be taken from him if he made himself obvious to the white people's eyes, kept him out of their sight. He dodged when he saw either one approaching.
>
> Mose considered the little boy beneath his notice and never gossiped to Lane, Senior, about the doings of the servants if it did not repay him in any way or avenge a seeming wrong.
>
> Sorrow they did not experience in that household, because each was sunk in upon himself to the extent that excluded

interest in anyone or anything not directly touching him. The gorgeous creatures were ever trying to make themselves seem more gorgeous and did not realize the needs of other people. The population at large as well as events, even, served as a background for their activities. Benjamin Lane, Senior, and his wife were gorgeous creatures.

The moment that fashions decreed anything new, they made a mad scramble for it even though it was sheer waste of time. In a way, this waste of time was a good thing, since it filled in their otherwise empty little lives.

Boy moved with the baby outside the gorgeous circle. He ordered the servants to give him things, which were always for the baby and not for himself.

After awhile, the grandmother took over and got all the needs filled. She was very conscientious, once she got started. In her acrimonious way, she possessed tenderness which she lavished on her grandson and on the little colored slave. The fact that the other servants feared her wrath, but loved her at the same time, made it easier for her to be obeyed.

Boy always held his ground before her. These two weaklings were as an immovable object resisting an irresistible force. Combined, they made a bulwark of strength that gave the baby the most wonderful start imaginable in life.

The arrogant old dame contributed to the molding of Boy's character, as well. She taught him, while she was teaching her grandson, to be sure, when he was old enough to understand, all the arts and graces of being a perfect gentleman. She also taught both of them to read and write. Obviously she taught her grandson, and unwittingly she taught the slave boy.

The whole countryside awoke to the fact, eventually, that the Lanes had an unusually brilliant son, but that time was still distant. What mattered now was the everyday task of living.

Almost overnight, disturbance occasioned by the arrival of such an important personage as the heir of these wealthy estates was either forgotten or relegated to the half-forgotten segment of the brain of all concerned. Around the house were so many sounds such as the tramp of horses' hooves on the gravel, the barking of dogs, the creak of carriages, the voices of the inhabitants raised in glee, pain, or anger. All these blended into a cacophony of sound that persisted throughout the day and to a lesser extent throughout the night, so that the occasional thin wailing of one infant in the reaches under the roof was amalgamated and dispersed in the general prevailing tone peculiar to the Lane house, and escaped notice.

Only the three who lived up near the roof did not care for the general run of aristocrats who frequented the Lane household off and on. They were far enough away physically as well as mentally, to see them as they really were. Grandmother Lane was old enough to have gained the experience of judging character. Boy grew into a nuisance and was treated as such by both blacks and whites, which experience gave him an instant education and unerring ability to evaluate which ones could or would hurt him.

It is very important to understand these two who brought up the baby since they influenced and molded the character of the heir of the Lane estates to such an extent that he was what he became through this influence.

After I finished writing, I thought very deeply about how I was hearing the words inside of me. It was as if I were reading aloud out of a book and putting down what I was reading.

As I was sitting on my window seat and watching a robin watching me from a branch on a level with my window, I felt such a wonderful peace come over me. Everything outside got all bathed in a golden glow and each leaf, butterfly, the robin and I were trembling with a life that was so big that it took in everything—the world, the sun, the moon, the stars—everything, everything and it was all one big whole that belonged together as one life. It seemed like something inside of me reached out and grasped all there was.

I did not know how long the feeling lasted. But, gradually, I seemed to be getting smaller and smaller and coming back to myself inside of my body from the vast outside, and my brain inside my head could not understand all that there was out there. But, I knew with no doubts that there was a part of me that knew everything and was part of that great life of which the world is only a very small, and not very important, part.

And then I got to thinking that it was only a month until I had to go back to school, and I would be a senior. I was not happy about that because I did not like school. My mind was made up about not doing so much of Eda's homework. Most of my spare time was spent in libraries all during high school. And that is how I discovered what a big treasure Uncle Eric's library was right under our own roof. He even had a catalogue that he showed me how to work, so that I could find any book I needed. And I made up my mind that I was going to do a lot of reading in his library downstairs.

He had so many of all kinds of books in the library that I got into reading by coming across them in the catalog. Specially I wanted to see if there were any books about ghosts because of Percy. And

I found a whole section of them listed under "PSYCHIC PHENOMENA". And some of the books made me understand a little bit about the things I saw and heard that other people could not. And those books were under "MYSTICISM". But the most interesting section was under "PHILOSOPHY". I found fascinating the books on people's remembrances of having lived before. My goodness! But that was so interesting and exciting to read. It made me wonder if I had ever lived before.

All that afternoon Aunt Cora was busy in getting a really nice dinner ready for another professor and his wife, whom Uncle Eric had invited. I helped her when she told me what to do. It was such a warm day that we had all the windows and doors open, so there was a nice breeze blowing through the house even if it was hot outside. And Aunt Cora had made me set the table with all glass dishes—the plates, the cups and saucers—everything was glass and it looked so cool. The water goblets were glass, too, of course, but had green leaves painted on them. The table looked so cool and beautiful with the white linen and the silver knives, forks, and spoons.

When the doorbell rang, Aunt Cora asked me to let the guests in.

"You must be Thelma," was the first thing the little man with the thick eyeglasses said when I opened the door. He had such a kindly face and a most unexpectedly deep musical kind of voice.

I nodded.

"I am Mrs. Nolan," his wife said to me. I held out my hand and she took it in both of hers and kissed my cheek.

"You are so beautiful!" she went on and stood back to look at me. She tilted her head first on one side, then on the other. I felt myself blushing and then they all laughed.

Mrs. Nolan was so tiny like a doll. Her movements were quick and she had a breathless way of talking. One would expect her to fly off any minute. Even when she was standing still, she gave the impression of just lighting for a moment.

"This is heavenly!" Mrs. Nolan looked around the dining room after Aunt Cora and Uncle Eric led them in. "How nice and cool it is here. I swear I have been sweltering all day in this awful heat."

We had a lovely dinner of all cool foods—vichyssoise, a molded salmon salad, and a lemon parfait.

And after the dinner, Aunt Cora and Uncle Eric and their guests went out to sit near the fountain out in the garden, while I did the dishes. Just when I was finishing, Uncle Eric came in to fix a big pitcher of mint juleps with no alcohol and I helped him with carrying out the tray and the glasses.

Professor Nolan taught philosophy and I was so interested in the things he said at dinner that I almost forgot to eat the wonderful salmon salad entree when he was talking about Oriental religions.

As Uncle Eric and I came outside, he was saying, "The fact of the matter is that the majority of the people in the world believe in reincarnation. They take it for granted. The only religions which do not have reincarnation as part of their beliefs, is Hebraism and Christianity. The common denominator underlying all, however, is the teaching that man's soul is immortal."

"It seems to me," Uncle Eric said, "that the greatest stumbling block to the acceptance of reincarnation, Professor Nolan, is that people do not remember their past lives."

Something seemed to pop into my mind all of a sudden when Uncle Eric said this. It was something I had forgotten completely. I remembered how one time during the summer I was sitting on my window seat and looking out at the tree and how the sun made patterns on the leaves and then I began thinking of the very first thing I could remember in my life. I went back and back and back. The more I could remember, the farther back I went. And then all of a sudden, I remembered something. It seemed that I woke up and thought, Oh, Lord, another day. How am I going to live through it.

I remembered about being a baby now; however, as a baby when I woke up, I did not know that I was a baby. I seemed to have some great and awful thing on my mind. Some sort of a big problem that I did not know what to do about. Then I thought I should get up, but as much as I tried I could not raise myself. Then I concentrated on raising my arm. My arm just jerked up and when I turned my eyes to it, I saw a baby hand. Then, I realized that I was a baby.

Oh, Lord, I thought, I am a baby. I wonder who my mother is.

Then I felt a sense of relief and gladness that I was a baby living another life. And I also had the memory of that awful previous life which was so filled with troubles, bigger than I could live through. I knew then that I had died in that other life and now I was a baby once more. I thought to myself that I had a great big secret that nobody else knew. But I knew. And I said to myself that I must not forget this great big secret and every time I wake up in my baby body, I will make myself remember that I had been born again.

And now as I sat beside Aunt Cora, I tried very hard to remember the rest of it, but in spite of my trying, I could not remember anything else. But I knew it was there, though, somewhere in my memories, way, way far back along with my baby memories even before I could talk. Thinking so hard made my head ache.

Then I became aware that everybody had stopped talking and they were looking at me. They were all smiling and I just looked around at them very puzzled.

"Professor Nolan asked you something," Aunt Cora said.

"I'm sorry. I was thinking," I blurted out. So everybody laughed.

"We were talking about extra-sensory perception," Uncle Eric explained. "And Professor Nolan asked what you thought about it."

I just wanted to get away and did not feel like being sociable any more. So I got up and said, "Please excuse me. I have a headache."

They all made sympathetic noises and I left.

Up in my room, I sat on the window seat, and looked out into the hot evening. The leaves were making a rustle every so often, but for the most part it was still and quiet outside. I tried remembering that baby memory once more, and anything about my former life. But, much as I tried, I could not remember anything else. After awhile I undressed and went to bed, thinking that maybe I could get an answer in my sleep. I concentrated all my thought on my baby memory and after awhile I fell asleep.

In the next few weeks before school started again, I thought about that first memory practically every night before I went to sleep. The only additional remembrance I got was my thinking at that time that my life was filled with weeping and that someone was after me for something all the time. The only peace I had was in sleep, and how wonderful it would be to wake up some day and find that all my troubles are gone. And when I discovered that I was a baby again, I was so thankful that I had left that trouble and nobody could reach me to make me miserable any more. But the thought kept nagging at me. Who had I been in that other life? What had been so awful about it? Who was it that caused my unhappiness?

And so I kept puzzling and wondering about it until I would get a headache.

And one day, it seemed to me that my very inner being spoke to me and said it would be too painful to recall and it would be better for my own benefit to look into the future and do the best I can each day. The past has given its lessons like going to school and learning how to fit oneself for living the best kind of life possible. And I ought to be satisfied to know that each person comes back again and again. It was not just something I read in a book or that somebody told me. I knew this for a fact.

Then, I thought of the story in the Bible that we had at Sunday School, about Lot's wife turning to look back and being changed into a pillar of salt. That story had more meaning for me. I gave up on trying to recall my past life and felt that I ought to concentrate on doing the best I could with this one.

Chapter 10

Starting school again in September was not so hard. In fact the subjects seemed so much easier. But, once more, I found myself as busy as ever and helping Eda with her homework, too, which I promised myself I would not do.

And it was all because Eda got so busy after school started, to get me elected Senior Class President. I did not particularly want to be president, because I thought that I just was not smart enough and besides that, I was a girl, and nobody wanted a girl to be Class President. But that did not stop Eda. She worked very hard at it and cried like everything when I was elected only vice-president.

So what else could I do when she asked me to help with her homework. I must have been a good teacher to her so far because she always used to pass all her tests and was a "B" student which was more than she could have done by herself, she kept telling me.

And now we were into October and Lucille was getting married in a few days.

On the day of her wedding, I woke up hearing the chime and reached for my notebook and pencil and started to write:

> Benjamin Lane, Junior, after uttering his first cry, went calmly to sleep. He stirred every now and then upon being bathed by the midwife but slept on until deposited in Boy's arms outside the bedroom door. His mother went right to sleep, also, from sheer relief now that those terrible pains were gone.
>
> Boy stood looking at the red infant whose little puckered mouth was working. Having seen animals born and being fed

from the teats of their mothers, he turned back to the door of the bedroom, but only for an instant. He turned back as his mind worked swiftly to where to find a teat for the baby. He remembered the Negress with the twins, whom she was still nursing and away he sped to suckle his treasure at the copiously flowing fount of the kindly woman, who occasionally nursed other babies, as well as her own.

Boy, clutching the light bundle, slid swiftly on silently padding feet through the house and out the back way. He darted beyond the stables, carriage house, and on to where the shanties stood which housed the slaves. He stopped at one of them and pushed open the door.

"Who dah?" the big booming voice of Sam, who had no rightful business to be there, spoke up belligerently.

Boy was not surprised. He saw and knew the promiscuity in which the slaves lived. As long as they did their work and did not hurt each other in any way that prevented them from working, they were left to themselves.

The master of the estate was too engrossed in pursuing pleasure at the moment, and left the running of it to his secretary. Fortunately for him, his Quaker secretary was a capable, scrupulously honest man in his dealings both with master and slave.

For erring slaves, punishment consisted of being locked up on bread and water for not more than three days. There was never any flogging or other cruel punishment. Consequently, no slaves ever ran away and their lot was happier than on many other estates. They came and went without too much supervision, therefore were a lot more loyal and reasonably honest, as far as a slave can be under the circumstances. And this manner of handling slaves was instituted by Lane, Senior's mother when she was mistress of the estate.

Naturally, the news that Boy brought the master's son to Lorie to nurse became known practically immediately. It was not an unusual event. As a matter of fact, it was commoner than realized to have white babies nursed by Negro slaves.

After Boy pushed open Lorie's door, he stood beside it and waited for Sam to get out of bed. Then, he extended the white baby to Lorie, who started nursing him immediately. Big Sam stood at the foot of the bed, waiting for Lorie to finish so he could resume whatever he had been doing.

The prior claim of the white master was thus served. No questions were asked and no answers given. The slow measure of breathing and the baby's feeding noises were the only sounds heard. The people did not seem to actually think. All three just waited.

Sam stood beside the bed which was a mat spread out on the dirt floor. Boy stood just inside the door where he had stepped back when he gave the infant to Lorie. Lorie lay on her side and held the infant who pulled at her breast. Her twins lay behind her near the wall.

The feeding process over, Lorie sat up and held out the baby and Sam waved his hand at Boy to take the baby away, which he did. He turned back toward the house and walked without making a sound. The baby slept.

The night was brilliant with stars. No moon was visible. Only transparent gauzy wisps of clouds scudded swiftly across the sky.

Boy glanced warily to either side of the driveway into the thick bushes. He never lost his fear of the night. Yet, he felt braver because of the sleeping bundle in his arms. He continued on to the dark silent house. No one was stirring now.

Boy, through force of habit, came in through the slaves' entrance and huddled against the wall as he climbed the stairs up to the empty kitchen as was his wont. He did not belong in any of the cabins. He slept where he could and when he could. He lay down under the large table in the kitchen, now. That is how the future master of this vast and wealthy estate spent his first night, sleeping in the arms of the only human being who wanted him.

With the coming of morning, the baby stirred in Boy's arms. Back to Lorie went Boy with the baby. Sam was gone by then and she was nursing her own offspring as she sat on the doorstep. Boy silently extended the baby and she laid aside one of her own, who started to object very loudly at having his meal interrupted so suddenly. A cow lowed complainingly in back of the shack. Lorie fed the white baby.

The wailing rightful heir to the fount of warm milk was restored to the nipple when the white baby had had its fill.

How enough milk issued out of Lorie to provide for her two infants, and now for the white baby, as well as various other black babies here and there, now and then, was a source of curiosity to Boy. Lorie's body was thin, yet her breasts were large and round. She milked the cow in back of her shack and sent up about half the milk to the house. The rest she used for herself and a few select favorites, mostly men. She even said once that she had nursed Boy when he was a baby. She never refused him a cup of milk when he asked for it. When he asked who his mother was, she became very angry and said that Boy's mother had died when he was born and never to ask her again about it. Once in awhile he caught Lorie looking at him curiously and when she got angry, she would kick out at him and tell him to go away because he did not belong.

And this morning, after the baby was fed, Boy took him and stepping into the bushes, merged with the growth and became invisible. He stepped out of the trees in front of the house and marched up the front stairs, through the open doorway and into the cool front hall. No one was about. There were noises here and there, some muffled and distant, some sharp and clear from nearby rooms. For the most part, the house still slept.

The Haunted House

I read over what I had written and marvelled that I could be writing about something I knew absolutely nothing about. Where out of my subconscious was all this coming?

A knocking on my door brought me out of my thoughts and it was Aunt Cora, telling me that breakfast was ready and we should be getting started for the wedding.

Then she went over to Johnnie's door and told him the same thing. Johnnie called out that he was up already and would be right down.

Johnnie had come home yesterday and he was very glad to see us all, just as much as we were to see him. He had missed us so much that he had even slept in his old room instead of going to the carriage house where he had fixed himself a place.

Yesterday afternoon, we all went for a rehearsal at the church where Lucille met us along with her bridesmaids, and Ben Lane. There was also Ben's accountant who was one of the ushers as well as Johnnie who was asked to be the other usher. All of us stood in the receiving line except Aunt Cora, so Ben Lane decided that she could be his adopted mother for the time being and so she got into the line, too. We had a lot of fun at the rehearsal and then went over to Lucille's house and had a very nice supper that she and her mother fixed.

And when we got home after the rehearsal and the supper, Johnnie and Uncle Eric talked a long time about the war that got started in September in Europe when the Germans invaded Poland. Johnnie kept saying that America would get into it, but Uncle Eric kept saying that we would give the Allies supplies but we would not send any soldiers. So they argued, and I could still hear them through the closed door after I went to bed.

And here it was the wedding day and I was not the least bit excited. In fact, I felt somehow sad. I tried to push the feeling away, but it stayed sort of on the edge of my consciousness even though I was busy thinking something else.

I looked at my maid-of-honor dress hanging in my closet and wondered when I would be looking at my wedding dress. Aunt Cora really made the dresses more beautiful than the pattern was. I remembered how Aunt Cora set out to be very stylish right after she married the professor, which is what we all used to call Uncle Eric. Anyway, once Aunt Cora made her mind up about something, she did it right. She used to have Johnnie bring magazines like Vogue and Harper's Bazaar from the library soon as they could circulate and she would study them from cover to cover. And she made all of her own clothes and cut the patterns from newspapers, then made them fit.

And that is how I got to wearing the latest style dresses made of the most fashionable fabrics. Sometimes, Aunt Cora would try out a style on me to see how it would look, and then she would change it a little bit for herself and maybe make something for herself in another color. In this way I got to wearing dresses that were a little too old sometimes for me, but it made me feel elegant.

Uncle Eric and Johnnie were glued to the radio, listening to the war news when I came down for breakfast, and Aunt Cora was busy fussing over everything and all of us to make sure that we all got ready on time.

After breakfast, I was still upstairs when I heard Johnnie and Uncle Eric go downstairs while Aunt Cora and I were dressing. They were all ready and called to us to hurry up. Uncle Eric then went to bring the Reo, which he had just bought, around to the front of the house.

Johnnie was standing near the door at the foot of the stairs and looking into the library when I came down. He looked so nice in his usher's clothes. He turned from staring into the library and looked at me. He got a peculiar look on his face as if he saw me for the very first time. My dress was a grown-up kind and Aunt Cora had helped me put up my hair and we had put some powder and lipstick on me to make me more grownup to match my dress. Johnnie tilted his head first to one side then to the other. I felt my face go red and got mad at myself for blushing.

Johnnie whistled. "Golly, Moses! You're grown up! Hey, Thelma, you sure are a knock-out!"

I felt awfully glad to hear him say it. Then, he came over and put his hand under my chin to make me look at him, and I didn't want to. My heart was going real fast. I wriggled away, and was glad that Aunt Cora started coming down the stairs. She looked so lovely in her blue dress and hat.

I did not know what was the matter with me all during the wedding ceremony. I was paying only half my attention to it, and the other half was on Johnnie. I had never before been so very aware of him in such a disturbing way. And I could not explain it to anybody, least of all to myself.

And the funny part of it was that whenever I happened to glance in his direction, I saw that he was looking at me. Sometimes he winked, but most often he just smiled.

I don't know how he managed it, but I rode back to the Lane

house in his roadster with Eda on the other side of me and the other two bridesmaids in the rumble seat.

The reception line was at the Lane house and everyone came along to kiss the bride and the young guys were even kissing the bridesmaids. Somehow Johnnie worked his way from the end of the line to where I was standing and in all the excitement and everybody kissing everybody else, Johnnie turned toward me in the receiving line and kissed me, too. Just before his lips touched mine, I saw his eyes go very dark, and my knees buckled. If he had not caught me up tight to himself, I might have sat down on the floor right there. My goodness, I though to myself, why do I get like this?

"What's the matter, Bunny?" Johnnie's lips brushed my ear as he whispered the question and I stopped breathing.

"I— I guess I'm tired of s-standing," I managed to whisper back.

By that time everybody was finished with the receiving line and people were starting to get their plates filled with food and glasses filled with whatever they wanted to drink.

Mrs. Seliski brought her accordian and Pasco Guidice brought his mandolin. One of the bridesmaids could play jazz on the piano real good, and pretty soon everyone was dancing and eating and drinking.

I kept looking around for Eda now and then but she did not seem to be around. And then I caught sight of her way over near the stairway leading upstairs and she seemed in deep conversation with Stephen. His blond head was very close to her dark one, and I wondered if they would start up another flirtation, only it was not a flirtation on her part from the very first.

I danced a lot, but the only one that I was feeling their arms around me was Johnnie's.

Then it started raining outside very hard and there was lightning and thunder, so all the Polish people went to Lucille and said that she was going to be very, very rich because there was rain on her wedding day. And by this time, it was evening.

Aunt Cora and Uncle Eric were having a wonderful time, but Ben just stuck around Lucille and only danced with Aunt Cora and me and Mrs. Grant. And Mrs. Grant danced with Pasco Guidice, which was kind of funny because he was a couple of inches shorter than she was.

Sometime during the evening, Eda brushed past me while dancing and said to me in a loud whisper, "Stephen is going to war."

Shortly after, people started going home, but we had to stay, and I felt very tired. Eda caught the bride's bouquet, of course, as I somehow knew she would.

Then, I became aware of Stephen hanging around near me but there was always someone with me, and he looked as if he wanted to talk to me.

So I excused myself and went over to him, and asked, "Do you want to talk to me?"

"Yes, but you're so popular that nobody can get to you."

I made some sort of silly remark and waited for him to tell me what was on his mind.

"Thelma, I want you to know that I am going to Canada to enlist in the Polish flying squadron. They are being trained in Canada."

"Must you?"

"Yes, I must. I come from an ancient titled family that fought all through the centuries. Even with King Sobieski at the time that they stopped the Turks from taking over Europe. I am a direct descendant of a long line of warrior knights that fought in every battle that Poland was ever engaged in."

I nodded because I could follow his line of reasoning, but I could not really understand it. I had the instant thought that his going would be so futile. As I looked at his face, I could not help noticing how haunted his eyes looked in spite of his self-possessed manner and cocky way of talking. I sensed that life scared him and he was fighting not to let anyone know how petrified he really was. In a way, it seemed to explain why he kept getting girls crazy about him, because it must have given him a sense of conquest. He was very handsome in a tall, blond way.

He leaned closer to me and said very low, "I want to make sure before I go that I leave an heir to carry on the family name and title."

I backed away and my eyes opened wide.

He followed me and went on. "After my training is done in Canada, I will come home on leave, and will get married to Eda, because she is the only girl who really loves me. I asked her tonight and she said she would. But, we have to elope and she wants you to help us. She wanted me to ask you."

I almost yelled, "What?" when Stephen first said that he was going to marry Eda, but clapped my hand over my mouth. And when he said that he wanted me to help them elope, I almost shrieked again.

"I have to think about it," I managed to say as I walked with him and Eda, who had joined us, to the door.

It had stopped raining and the street lamp was reflected brightly in the puddles of the walk leading back around the house to the lane. As Stephen jumped over a large puddle, his arms stretched out wide and for an instant, his body became a cross which was reflected on the walk by his shadow cast by the lamp. I felt as if a cold hand closed over my heart and squeezed it.

Eda turned to follow him and called over her shoulder. "My grandmother thinks I'm spending the night at your house."

"Oh, no," I whispered to myself and tears rushed into my eyes.

I woke up in the middle of the night and lay listening for what had awakened me. Then I heard a ping sound as if something hit the pane of my open window. After awhile, it came again, so I got up and went over to the window and looked down.

I heard Eda's loud whisper, "Let me in."

So I went downstairs very quietly, but had a flashlight as I didn't want to run into any furniture, and went to the side door of the living room where there was a roof extension over the driveway. Eda and Stephen were both there, and Stephen whispered to me, "Take care of Eda for me!" and melted into the darkness.

Oh, dear! I thought to myself. Why me? What am I going to do now?

Eda and I crept into my room without making a sound and her clothes were soaked through to the skin. She was lucky that it was still pretty warm with its being Indian summer, or she would have caught pneumonia for sure. I gave her one of my pajamas and we spread out and hung up all her clothes to dry.

"Where were you and how did you get so wet?" I wanted to know.

"Up on Stephen's roof making love and everything was wet."

My mouth dropped open. "Really making love?" was all I could say.

"Yes!" and she looked straight at me and large tears started rolling down her face but she was not making a sound—no sobbing, no crying, no nothing—only huge, shining, tears rolling down her cheeks and dropping onto the pajama jacket.

I grabbed her shoulders and shook her fiercely for the first time since I had known her when we were both little kids.

"Why?" I asked angrily.

"He may die, and I want to have his baby. Thelma, I love him, and I can't stop."

"Can't you wait till you marry him? Oh, no! You cannot marry him after all. You are not old enough, and you have to have your mother's permission. Eda! What are you going to do?"

Eda got a stubborn look on her face. "He's going away tomorrow. I mean today— this morning, when it gets light. And I didn't want to lose him in case he finds another girl in Canada."

"Oh, Eda! You must be absolutely crazy! So what if he does find somebody else, and you already spoiled!"

"I don't care. And if I have a baby, it will be his."

"What will your mother say?"

"What can she say? She had me before she married my father."

"Who's your father?"

"Captain Olafsen."

"Isn't it funny, but I always thought there was something about you that reminded me of the captain, but you look mostly like your mother."

"So what can she say? I am old enough to get married, anyhow."

"No, you are not."

"Yes, I am. I always lied by one year when I went to school, because I was little and could not speak good enough English to start school. All I could speak was Italian. My mother worked hard with me for a year so I could learn to speak English enough to go to school, and when I went to school, a year was taken off my age. But, I have my baptismal certificate to prove that I am eighteen. Only you know this— and God," she added.

"And your mother," I reminded her.

"And my father," she concluded.

"So what about eloping if Stephen shows up after the training is over?"

"We'll get married some way, even if we have to go to Connecticut."

Another thought struck me. "Oh, Eda! Suppose you are going to have a baby, and it starts showing, and Stephen does not come back. What about school and graduation?"

"I don't care."

With that we both got into bed and I fell asleep once more, wondering how I would explain Eda's presence in the house, when everybody knew that she had not come in with us last night.

I woke up again when it was just beginning to get daylight and everything was so still and just beginning to be visible. And I woke up with the awful thought that Stephen could not elope or even get married without his father's permission because he was not of age. And I also wondered if he would be taken into training in Canada if he were not of age. But my biggest worry right now was that he could not marry Eda on his own, so I shook her awake and she was smiling and saying, "Stevie," very softly.

Then I knew that she really loved him in a grownup way, and was not merely in love with him. Still the heavy pinched feeling in my heart was there when I thought of Eda and Stephen together.

I kept shaking her until she sat up and was awake.

I whispered, "Eda, listen hard, please! It is important. Stephen cannot marry you without his father's signing a paper because he is not of age. So you cannot elope and marry secretly. You can, but he cannot. And I don't know if he can get into training in Canada because of his age."

She pulled her knees up and stared at me. "What am I going to do?"

"Well, you better catch him and talk to him before he gets on the bus today. What time is he leaving?"

"I don't know," she said in a small voice.

So, we both dressed in my clothes because hers were still wet, and went downstairs very quietly. I wrote a note to Aunt Cora that I was going to Eda's with something she forgot, which was true in a way, and tacked it up on the board near the sink. Then, we both let ourselves out and ran to the back gate and through Lucille's garden and sat under the lilac bush to watch Stephen's door. I was glad that I thought of bringing some sweaters and a half a loaf of bread because we got kind of cold and very hungry.

After a long while we saw Pasco Guidice come to the corner and stretch and look around, so we knew it was eight o'clock because that was when he opened his store on Sunday. He opened it after eight because he went to first Mass. That's what Eda told me. Weekdays he opened the store at seven in the morning, and closed it at nine, except Sunday when he closed it at one in the afternoon.

Pretty soon there were kids and mothers running to the store and running back home. It was Sunday so people were sleeping late.

And then we saw Mr. Seliski coming out and Stephen was following him. I grabbed Eda and pulled her to come after me. She sort of hung back when she saw that Stephen's father was with him.

And so we followed them to the bus station and caught up when Mr. Seliski was buying the ticket for Stephen. When Stephen saw us come up, he got a scared look on his face and then I knew in a flash that going to Canada was all his father's idea. Other thoughts tumbled over one another in my head. I knew that the father was the kind of person who always wanted to do things through others. Like pretending he could not walk so he could get half-pay and Stephen's mother had to take in washing for them to live on. And now he was pushing Stephen to go to war and maybe get killed because he was a patriot. Well, if he was an honest-to-God patriot, he should go himself. With that I got mad.

I don't know where the words came from but they came out fast and angry. "Mr. Seliski," I said. "Eda and I came to the station to say goodbye to Stephen because Eda and Stephen want to get married and they love each other. They cannot wait because Stephen may get killed in the war and he is the oldest one to carry on the Seliski name. He may not even come back from training because there are all sorts of dangers in learning to fly. So we came to say goodbye in case he does not come back, if you don't let them get married."

Eda and Stephen were standing apart as I faced the father. All sorts of expressions crossed his face. Surprise at first, then anger, surprise again, and finally a defeated kind of look as if he thought of something that had never occurred to him before.

He grabbed Stephen's shoulder and asked something in Polish very angrily and Stephen nodded. The father shot out his hand and slapped Stephen so hard that Stephen reeled and almost fell but Eda grabbed him.

Then Eda made a kind of animal sound from deep in her throat—a raging sound like a growl but mixed with a wail—a sound like I never heard before in my life and shot past me to hurl herself at the father. Both of them fell with Eda on top, who kept up that awful shriek and she was raking the man's face with her nails, and beating at him with her body and legs. It took the combined strength of Stephen and another man to pull her off. She was in hysterics and yelling in Italian mixed up with English all kinds of awful things that I could only guess at.

Mr. Seliski scrambled up and there was blood on his face. He ran off as fast as he could. I saw Stephen start after him. Then he stopped. He turned around and came back to Eda. He smoothed her hair and wiped her tear-stained face with his hands and held her close to his chest until her wild sobbing evened out into whimpers.

I heaved a big sigh of relief to see Stephen become a man in just a few seconds. And then I knew for a fact that it takes a woman to make a man out of a boy, after she gives herself to him.

After awhile Eda lifted her head up and asked, "What are we

going to do, Stevie?"

"We have to go tell your grandmother everything first," he said and picked up his suitcase.

Somehow I had a sure and positive feeling at that moment that I had saved Stephen's life but did not know how exactly.

We walked uptown again and they turned off on the avenue while I continued on home.

I felt so tired and sleepy. Everybody was having breakfast and listening to the war news, and Aunt Cora only asked if I had breakfast at Eda's. I said, "No," so she filled a plate for me and I ate. Then I went upstairs and got into bed again.

Chapter 11

The story about the baby and Boy came more and more often until I was writing practically every day. This evening all of my homework was done, so I went back to where I started writing regularly and re-read what I had written to date:

> Seemingly, the order of the house was not disrupted in any way by the arrival of the infant. When someone saw Boy with the infant, he remembered that there was a baby son of the household, and promptly forgot it until the next time.
>
> Boy thought that he must get a room in the mansion. His method was not to ask for a room for himself, but to demand one for his master. To his own surprise, it worked. He accosted Benjamin Lane, Senior's valet-butler-general informer Mose as he was issuing out of his own master's bedroom, and gave his command. The man cast one glance at the infant in Boy's arms and waved his hand in a vaguely upward direction, murmuring something about an "Ol' nuh'se'y upstaihs" and went on to get the breakfast tray.
>
> Boy knew which stairs led up because he had spent many a cold night on the stairs huddled against a warm wall close to a chimney and had stolen quietly away long before everybody else was up. Yet he had never ventured to the top or explored the regions beyond the head of the stairway.
>
> Now, he held the infant before him as the opener of all doors and went up the stairs boldly.
>
> The household, with the exception of Grandmother Lane,

was still abed when Boy climbed the stairs to reach the old nursery. The old woman heard the creaking of the stairs near the top and thought it was the slatternly Mandy heaving her bulk to bring the breakfast. Usually, the grandmother hobbled down to breakfast, but on the mornings that she did not appear, Mandy brought it to her. But, the creaking came much faster than that made by Mandy. She opened the door and stood on the threshold. Her eyes fell on the small colored boy she saw often around the house and grounds and knew his begetting. She had more than an ordinary interest in the child, and scrutinized him sharply periodically to see how much of the white in him was cropping out. Now she saw that he was holding an infant in his arms.

She remembered the disturbances of the previous night.

The awkwardness of the long pause with the old woman standing in the doorway of her room and Boy with his charge at the head of the stairs was broken by the old lady. She stepped quickly toward the closed door of the room next to her's. She opened it and barked out, "Come in! Don't stand there! This is the nursery. Tell that blackguard good-for-nothing Mose to get a cradle in here!

"No! Don't take the baby!" She shrieked quite oblivious to the fact that there was no place to put the infant down. "Leave the baby here!"

But Boy was down the stairs already, yet heard her scolding following him.

I stopped for a minute and wondered at how the story jumped around. It did not follow time like it does for everybody from day to day and so on from year to year. It went back and forth like someone tells a story and keeps remembering things that had been omitted at the beginning, and keeps filling in the empty spaces. It seemed kind of funny, but I was so interested that I did not mind. I went on reading.

The old woman's nagging was to be constantly in Boy's ears, but one thing may be said that she never struck Boy or her grandson. At times her verbal basting was worse than physical punishment. She was an expert.

Boy scrambled down the stairs in pursuit of Mose who had gone to the kitchen to have his own breakfast and to see what he could see. Boy caught up with him in the kitchen and demanded a cradle for his master.

Mose was annoyed. "Tell the othahs whut yuh wahnts. Ah'm buhsy, cain't yuh see? Is yo eyes closed?" he muttered.

From then on, Boy prefaced his demands with, "Mose says

he's busy. My master wants—" and he specified what was needed.

Now he went to look for the man-about-the-house who did all the hard work and always knew where everything was. This time he led Boy to another wing of the house where several rooms were not in use and where all the furniture, for which there was no further use, was standing in any which order. The cradle, covered with dust, was easily found.

Then Boy picked out all the pieces of furniture for which he felt there was even the remotest possibility of use. As Boy pointed out the pieces of furniture, the husky Negro carried them up to the garret room. Besides the cradle, there was a bed, a cot for himself, two chests of drawers (one large and one smaller), several chairs, a large table and two small ones, even a small desk, as well as a pile of rag rugs which had been rolled in a corner.

The nursery was very large, spreading as it did, over two-thirds of the house. The small room next to it, which Grandmother Lane occupied comprised the rest of the attic. In the nursery there were windows all around and no walls to close out the sunlight.

Of course, the furniture was covered with the dirt and dust of years, but Grandmother Lane soon had several girls running about cleaning, washing, scrubbing and polishing everything. The furniture got pushed about a bit before getting located in just the right place to suit the old lady. This done, the nursery was the airiest and lightest room in the whole house. It swallowed up the many pieces of quite large furniture, yet was not crowded.

The old woman was very officious, and directed the work in progress in a tone of voice that kept the girls moving fast to get away from it.

Boy sat to one side holding the baby and disappeared every so often to have the infant fed or to change its wraps.

Elvira Lane's maid, who had made the baby's clothes, gave them all to Boy when he said that Mose was busy and clothes were needed for the baby.

And when he went to Lorie for the baby's feeding, she showed him how to bathe it. And she told Boy that white babies needed to be bathed very often, every day as a matter of fact, because they had a bigger stink.

When all the furniture was placed in the nursery, the grandmother had the cleaning squad with pail, rags, soap and water clean up the windows, walls and floor. There was no chatting and time wasting under her watchful eyes. Each did her work as directed. Each wanted to get away as soon as possible and hastened to finish it.

The walls were panelled in wood. Years ago, when she was mistress of the house, she could have had the walls papered with the French paper which was very fashionable then, but she liked the beauty of the natural wood which had been used.

Now she surveyed with satisfaction the simplicity that created a beautiful room which had not been used for about thirty years. Boy simply stood aside and waited till everything was finished and then took possession.

The old woman was really enjoying herself at long last. As time passed, she was careful not to obtrude too obviously on either her son or her daughter-in-law, fearing that they might interfere with, or even take her little kingdom away from her.

Faint repercussions reached the master and mistress of the house that Grandmother Lane had taken charge of their offspring which relieved them no end and kept them from disrupting their own order of activities. They were satisfied that everything was in order and further attention from them was not needed.

Mose felt it was beneath him to gossip about this phase of family life.

In this manner, the little household within the greater household, grew and developed independently until, in time, it blended and engulfed the greater household. When this happened, it became the center of an activity that changed the course and history of a nation.

The rooms at the top of the house eventually became the center of a new idealistic state growing into reality.

The old woman who was really responsible for all this, did not know how well she sowed her seeds nor how fruitful would be the harvest at the time that she instilled her ideas into the minds of her two charges. She was the real one who started the ball rolling for a new nation. No one really taught her the ideas she had. She arrived at her conclusions by her own reasoning.

In adulthood, Boy received his just reward and station. He became a free, respected and educated man who could read, write, and converse intelligently upon topics requiring keen observation, even extraordinary reasoning powers and a facility of thought management to draw logical conclusions. For a self-educated man, this was no mean accomplishment.

After I finished reading, the thought came to me that some day I would let Ben Lane read the story. And thinking of Ben Lane, made me think of Lucille, so I went downstairs and left a note on the board that I would be going to Lucille's and went out the back gate and through her mother's garden.

And this made me think of Pasco and the widow Perrutti. And thinking of the people in the block reminded me of Stephen and Eda, and how Stephen's father ran away from the bus station and when he got home, he packed a bag and told Mrs. Seliski that he changed his mind about Stephen's going and would go himself up to Canada. And here it was Thanksgiving next Thursday and nobody heard any more from him.

Well, Stephen went back to his home with Eda and I don't know what they told his mother, but she went with them to get the marriage license and they got married quietly in the reception room at the priest's house. I could not be her bridesmaid because I was a Protestant, so Stephen's sister, Mary, was the bridesmaid and Mrs. Crespi's oldest son, Danny, who lived on the first floor under the Seleskis, was the best man.

Eda wore her bridesmaid's dress again and she looked so beautiful. So it was true that she was next to get married because she caught Lucille's bouquet.

Eda's grandmother, along with Pasco Guidice, put up a big table in the room in back of his store by laying some boards across saw horses and covered it with a big sheet. There was lots to eat of all kinds of delicious Italian food and Eda's mother sent a big money order to the grocer to pay for everything, Eda told me.

It was a very quiet wedding, no music and dancing, because Stephen's father went away to war, everyone was told. Considering that everyone on the lane came to the wedding, it really amazed me that nothing was told beyond the block. Eda kept on going to high school and put her wedding ring on a chain inside her dress. She was captain of practically all the teams at school and I kept helping her with her homework and everything went on like it always had. But, I kept watching Eda if she were getting fatter, but she stayed her skinny energetic self.

I heard someone running in back of me as I was walking to Lucille's and I turned around to see Eda. She told me quickly that her mother-in-law got a letter from England and it was from Stephen's father. He said he had joined the Polish government in exile there. So Stephen was writing his father about the wedding and how he and Eda were living with Eda's grandmother but coming to visit his mother on the lane practically every day. And when we got to Lucille's, Eda told her the news.

After awhile, Lucille told us that she was pretty sure that she was going to have a baby, but would let us know when she was definite about it.

I felt Eda squeeze my hand and I opened my eyes wide when I looked at her, but she made a "no" shake with her head ever so slightly. Lucille did not notice it.

So we talked a little bit about Ben and Uncle Eric getting

together on a government contract to carry war supplies because Ben had been on ships such a long time and knew more about it than Uncle Eric. And now they were buying more ships. Then we were talking about submarines sinking ships and that made me worry. Uncle Eric and Johnnie were both away and sometimes we did not hear from them for days and days.

On the way from Lucille's, Eda told me that she and Stephen had been talking about Stephen's maybe going to work on Uncle Eric's ships, which would pay more perhaps than the foundry was paying him. It took practically all that he was earning and what his sister Mary was getting working in Grant's basement, to keep the household going at his mother's. He and Mary would not let her take in any more washing. As it was, the money Eda's mother sent to the grandmother supported Eda and Stephen and the grandmother. If it were not for that, Eda would have to quit school and go to work. So I told Eda that I would ask Uncle Eric about it as soon as he came home again from New York, where he had so much business that he had to take an apartment. Aunt Cora was pretty busy going back and forth between New York and Providence these days.

Seeing as I got an allowance last night, I invited Eda to come to the ice cream parlor on the avenue and get a banana split and maybe buy all the movie magazines. Eda was so happy about that because she could not get any more money just for fun things. Besides, I wanted to see if I could find anything in the magazines about my real father.

It was dark and quite late by the time we got finished with our banana splits, so Eda ran off home and I went home to read the movie magazines.

There was only one tiny paragraph in one of the magazines about Vern Framingham which said that the has-been silent's star was reported doing some directing in the experimental television studios in New York. I cut the little piece out to put in my scrapbook.

Then I sat in the dining room with Aunt Cora while she planned the Thanksgiving Dinner. Uncle Eric was coming from New York on Monday, and Johnnie was coming with Captain Olafsen and Eda's mother from San Francisco either on Monday night or Tuesday morning depending on trains from New York.

The Captain and Eda's mother were having dinner at the grandmother's and would meet their new son-in-law and his family. Which made me think that when Eda ever got her baby, it would be Italian-Swedish-Polish extraction. It could happen only in America, I guessed.

Chapter 12

It was Sunday after Thanksgiving that Johnnie asked me if I had written any more on the story that kept coming to me, so I gave him the notebooks into which I had copied my scribbles, and while he read, I copied the last couple of dictations:

> Boy naturally took advantage of opportunities as they came to him. This was an asset to his master, in the future, when he could thrash out his problems adequately with an intelligent being and was sure of advice which could actually be followed with good results.
>
> The same morning that Boy started the ball rolling toward establishing living quarters for his charge and himself, marked a great change in a good many lives. Sooner or later, everyone in the community was affected. The people would have scoffed at the mere idea of an elderly gentlewoman and one little black boy, working together, were having an effect on their lives. It was a peppery dame and one little black slave, but they had a little white baby and that is what made the vast amount of difference.
>
> No one could quite say in what way everything changed as the years passed, yet everyone assured everyone else that there had been a change. The only oblivious ones, who were responsible for this change, were the individuals comprising the tight little trio up near the roof of the Benjamin Lane house. The odd thing was that they had not much concern for the outside world, sunk in as they were upstairs upon their own little world.
>
> It was a week before the place started assuming a semblance of what it became later on. All the shelves of books had not made their appearance as yet, but they had their allotted space ready at Grandmother Lane's instructions in building them. All the walls had been scrubbed clean under the vigilant eyes of the old woman. Yet there were no feminine touches of fripperies about the place. She was too old to be vain and had lived long enough to get the broad view of comfort rather than the small fussy existence among

trinkets that really contributed nothing. Thus, the place became home and Boy moved in with the baby.

Boy was inwardly excited and amazed that so much good luck was coming to him on account of the baby. He clung to it and would hardly let anyone touch it.

The Lane household, permeated as it was with all the material emotions, thoughts and actions of its dwellers, had that one haven of peace and rest at the top of the house. Everyone else at the lower levels lived in an atmosphere of perpetual turmoil over conflicting reactions. Days and nights went in rapid succession filled with events of social importance.

The whirlpool of activity swirled around Elvira who was very busy making up menus, being fitted for dresses, and engaging in petty intrigues of clandestine assignations and even arranging flirtatious diversions between bored wives and willing, charming lechers. Matchmaking, of course, was a major activity of all the wives in the community. Parties, balls, teas, visits, and callings on each other filled the time completely.

All this happened below the foot of the nursery stairs, leading to almost another world.

Boy went to the Quaker for some clothes for himself. Because one day the grandmother looked at the child's dirty tattered shirt and very ragged breeches, then shrilled at him to repair to the overseer-secretary to get himself outfitted as befits a body servant to the heir of the wealthy estate.

The suddenness of this great good fortune left Boy speechless. He stood goggle-eyed. The mere idea of possessing brand new beautiful clothes—and stockings—and shoes!—left him without a coherent word to utter. It just could not be true.

Yet, here stood the old woman remonstrating at the top of her cracked voice for him to go and get all these things.

He was afraid of approaching the Quaker by himself and did not want to use Mose as an intermediary.

When the urgent voice of Grandmother Lane yelled out the order to begone and tend to the task, he caught up the baby and went down the stairs. The baby had been washed and dressed in very clean white clothes, so that the contrast between it and its bearer was more than marked.

Boy presented himself before the overseer. Of course, Quaker John knew that a baby boy had been born to the mistress of the house, but he had not seen it and, like everyone else, he had shut up the fact in a separate part of his brain. The fact was let out of the mental chamber, as it were, when Boy stood in front of him.

"They tole me it is fitten for my Master's boy to have clothes fitten." Boy said all he was going to say on the matter and stood still. The baby was making bubbling noises, his blue eyes roving and his little fists moving from side to side.

Quaker John pushed his chair back and strode toward Boy. Boy's impulse was to shrink but he conquered that involuntary movement with all the will power he could muster, and stood still as a rock. That was the greatest, or next to the greatest step forward which he took in his life. Never again, after this, did he shrink from anyone, white or black. This is how he started acquiring a deep and controlled sense of power.

As he stood, Quaker John came up and looked down very interestedly at the baby, his cynical mind trying to see whom the baby resembled—the husband or the mother, or neither. Boy did not take his eyes off the man's face. He stood and waited.

The man walked back to the desk, sat down and taking a piece of paper toward him, wrote rapidly with a scratching quill. Boy thought he was being ignored and that his request was for naught. Still he stood and waited. As he watched the man write, he felt that such an accomplishment was the most wonderful gift anyone could have. He did not realize that deep within his subconscious mind, the will had been born to learn to write when the opportunity presented itself.

Quaker John wrote a long time and finished with a flourish. He sealed the letter and got up. He traversed again the distance between his desk and Boy. He handed the letter to Boy and waved him out of the room. Not a word had been spoken by the man.

Boy shifted the baby to one arm and took the letter. The man had forgotten or was too preoccupied to realize that Boy could not read. Boy looked at the markings on the outside of the envelope and back at the overseer who had turned his back on Boy and walked away. Boy was at a loss what to do but knew that he was being dismissed and left. He trudged back up to the attic and held out the envelope to the grandmother who had greeted him with a tirade for taking the baby with him.

She peered at the envelope and swore a string of abuse at its writer.

"Here!" she gave the envelope back to Boy, "Give this to the tailor in the village."

It was then that Boy realized that he would get his clothes after all.

Since all the new clothes had to have measurements taken for them, it was very important that Boy go to the tailor immediately.

This time he did not take the baby with him. He ran to the village at top speed, the letter tightly clutched in his fist. Other tailors there were, but Boy chose the poorest one and walked into the shop.

"Hey, this is really exciting, Bunny!" Johnnie said after he read it all. "Pure stream of consciousness creativity, I would say. But which level of consciousness are you tapping?" he wanted to know.

"I don't understand what you mean, Johnnie."

"Well, never mind. Just keep on writing. Does anyone know about this?"

"No. Only you."

"That's good. Let's keep it that way for the present. Obviously there must be some connection with Mr. Lane's ancestors here. And you say that you were only speculating on how the name of our back street got its name when you started writing this story?"

"Yes."

"Isn't that something. You know, Bunny, I read somewhere once, I don't remember where, that everything happening is imprinted in some finer dimension, in ether I believe it was called, but I forget."

Johnnie was sprawled on my window seat and looking out into the garden. I was sitting cross-legged on the floor.

He continued, "I remember also something about some individuals being able to tap those sources, either backward or forward, because everything is there. The medium carrying these records is beyond time and space dimensions."

"I'm trying to understand what you are saying, Johnnie."

"It does not seem to be beyond the scope of understanding that we can go backward and forward in time. Consider the marvelous inventions that have come into being. The idea for them must be in existence, or else it would not have occurred to anyone. I sure wish I had some such ability to tap that source of ideas. I would like to know how this war will turn out, for one. We will get into it, Bunny. Mark my words. It is only a question of time."

"Do you think you will be in it?"

"I'm in it already and will probably get into the thick of it. And what do you think of it?"

"When I really pay attention to the news when it comes on the radio, I get a feeling that I am in the middle of a black whirling cloud from which terrible cries of pain are coming. There is a choking sensation, too, as if I cannot breathe. It is all so evil that I struggle to rise above it and imagine myself going into a ball of brilliant light and the awfulness stops."

And then we got to talking about Mr. Seliski going to England to be with the Polish government in exile. Johnnie thought that was a great and wonderfully courageous thing to do. I was sort of tempted to remind Johnnie all about Mr. Seliski pretending he could not walk and then about the miracle, and about his trying to send Stephen but Eda beat up on him, so he went himself. I was tempted, but I said nothing. It was as if I knew inside that I must never talk about anything or it would not turn out all right if there was anything wrong. Johnnie once said that I was something—but I could not remember the name until it popped into my head unexpectedly and the word was "catalyst". He said that somehow when I got mixed up in anything, it turned out all right. And I knew inside that I must never talk idly about it because talking created some sort of energy preventing the flow which was setting things right. To make things right, you had to go with the positive flow and not bring anything negative to interrupt or hinder the flow.

We heard the front door bell ring and pretty soon Uncle Eric stood in the open doorway of my room and said that Ben Lane came and wanted to talk business so Johnnie got up and went downstairs, while I asked Uncle Eric if Stephen could work for his company. Stephen needed more money to support his mother.

Uncle Eric was surprised that Stephen, being only eighteen years old, was doing all that supporting. Of course, a good job could be found for him, but it would mean moving away most probably if Ben Lane could not use him in his Providence office. He said to tell Eda to send Stephen over to talk about it before Tuesday because that was the day he would be going back to New York.

So then, as long as Ben had come over, I thought maybe Lucille would like some company, so I went through the back gate and over to the Lane house.

She was very glad to see me because she was making draperies for the odd room upstairs and needed help in putting them up. She thought she might fix it up like a study and one corner for her sewing things. I looked around and studied everything closely. Right square in the center of the room was a triangular raised small platform, and there was a long bench on each side of the room, built right into the wall. The room was more oblong than square and the benches were on both the long sides of the room, facing each other. And at the far end was a platform with three steps leading to it.

Lucille spoke, "I bet this room was used for some sort of assemblies and the raised platform was for the speaker. But the purpose of the triangular thing in the middle of the floor beats me."

I walked over to it and sat down on it. Lucille was busy putting up a hem and I sat watching her. Then, a low sound filled my ears that started out softly like, "Oooooooooommmmmmmmmm—" and got louder as if the whole room was filled with the sound. I jumped up and the sound stopped suddenly. After a while, I sat down again, and heard the same thing.

After I jumped up the second time, I called to Lucille, "Will you come over and sit down beside me on this little platform, Lucille, and tell me if you can hear anything."

So, she came over to sit down and as we plunked ourselves down, both at the same time, the little platform moved a little. And then we both jumped up at the same time and the platform moved some more. Without saying a word, we both bent down at the same time and shoved. The platform was heavy but it moved. We pushed with all our might and Lucille almost fell into the hole underneath.

She ran out to get a flashlight while I peered down into the hole. There was a built-in ladder leading down. The flashlight showed a small room down there filled with all sorts of things.

Lucille went first and I followed. We found ourselves in a place as big as a big closet.

Then we heard the front door slam and heard Ben calling, "Lucy, Where are you? Papa's home!"

"Here!" Lucille called back and we heard him run up the stairs and pause.

"Here! Ben!" Lucille called again and pretty soon Ben was looking down into our upturned faces.

"Well! Son-of-a-gun! What are you two doing down there?"

"Thelma and I discovered the hole in the floor and we just came down to explore when you came into the house."

"Just wait a sec. I'll go get a lantern so we can see better," and he ran out of the room and downstairs.

He was back almost immediately with the lighted lantern and came down the ladder to join us. There was hardly room for all of us but we squeezed by each other to examine things.

We saw a lectern and a triangular hollow box about as high as my waist and it obviously fitted onto the triangular platform above us. And there were small leather covered trunks and some hinged boxes around. A sword in a scabbard lay across one of the boxes. The hilt was all black, but there was a tiny bit of silver showing here and there so I guessed it needed some silver polish. I picked it up and pulled it out of the scabbard. And I felt a warm tingle go up my arm and touch my heart. The blade had some rust spots on it, but not many.

"Look, Ben," Lucille was saying, "There are folded cloths in this trunk."

She was taking out the unfolding silk cloths that had embroidered symbols on them — crosses, triangles and other things.

Ben was holding and examining candle holders. There were several of them, and one was a candelabra for three candles.

I put down the sword after I put it back in the scabbard and lifted the hinged top of the box on which the sword had lain. It was all full of all kinds of papers. Lucille came over and lifted up one batch to carry over to the lantern so she could see better.

"It is written in French, Ben," she said. "And here's one that's all in Latin."

Ben came over to stand near us. "Here's what I think," he said. "I think that the room above us was used as some sort of fraternity meeting place, and they kept their paraphernalia down here. But, what really puzzles me is that all this boxed space is not missed downstairs."

"It must be the space in back of the stairway," Lucille suggested. "From the living-room side there is a solid wall, and there is also a solid wall from the dining-room side."

"You are absolutely right, Lucy."

I thought to myself that our house, too, had a secret place under the front stairway.

Then I said, "My uncle is a Mason and maybe he can tell us for sure what these papers are. I will ask him if you want me to."

"Hey! That's a good idea," and Ben put all the papers back into the box and carried it up the ladder. There was another box that had some kinds of records in it, and he took that one up, too.

Then Ben rearranged all the things so there would be more room and as he was dragging a trunk over the floor, it caught on something, so he took a flashlight to see what it was, and it was a small ring in the floor. There had been a small fitted piece of wood over the hollowed out space where the ring was, but the wood must have warped because the bottom of the trunk jarred it loose. So Ben brought the lantern over and looked all around the space. He told Lucille to hold the lanter and he moved some more boxes aside.

"By gum! By golly! By jingo! It's a trapdoor! Stand aside everybody—" and he pulled the ring.

There was a lot of squeaking and groaning, but the door in the floor came up, and Ben took my flashlight to shine down the hole.

"Well, I'll be—," Ben knelt down to get a better look. "It's the storage closet in back of the shoe shop. That's where I keep all my junk."

He got up and shut the trap door. And as he turned to go up the ladder again and Lucille held up the lantern, we saw another ladder lying on its side against the wall. It was in back of the ladder that led up to the floor above.

"Aha! That's the ladder used to get down to the cellar," said Ben.

Once we were upstairs, Lucille said, "What beats me is all that secrecy. I wonder why?"

"Well, fraternal organizations tend to be secret, as a rule," Ben said.

"Yes, I know. But fraternal halls are all over the place, and there's nothing secret as far as their meeting places are concerned— The Masons, the Odd Fellows, the Knights of Columbus, Knights of Pythias, the Elks, the Moose— Well, anyway, there's no secret about their existence. I think this inn, way back then, was used for some other secret activity. I do."

"You may be right."

"And may I tell Uncle Eric all about our finding all this?"

"Oh, sure! Do that. His being a college professor, he can tell us in a jiffy what this is all about."

I ran as fast as I could back home through the Grant's garden and in our back gate. I was all out of breath when I got home, and Aunt Cora was having some sort of a tea or bridge club party or something that she got mixed up in with the faculty wives at Brown, so I stayed in the dining-room only long enough to be introduced to the ladies I had not met before and went into the library. Uncle Eric was in there with Johnnie. So I told them all about finding the hidden room under the floor and everything.

Uncle Eric got very excited and jumped up. He went out of the library and stuck his head inside the dining-room archway.

"Excuse me ladies—," he said, and to Aunt Cora, "am going over to Ben Lane's, my dear."

"May I go, too?" Johnnie asked.

"I would like to go, too," I added.

So Uncle Eric stuck his head in again into the archway and said, "Excuse me again— And the children want to come," he said to Aunt Cora.

Johnnie and I looked at each other when he called us "children", so everybody started to laugh and we went out to the kitchen and through the back gate. I was hoping Mrs. Grant was not home to see all the traffic through her garden. Uncle Eric was almost running, he was so excited.

Once more, Lucille, Ben and I went up to the meeting room with Uncle Eric and Johnnie following us. Uncle Eric went right over to the pile of papers, which had come out of the hinged box, and which Ben left on one of the side benches and which he pointed to when we came into the room.

Uncle Eric sat down and started reading the French papers first. He did not say anything to any of us. Then he read the Latin ones. We could see that he understood everything he was reading. I sat down on the floor in front of him and so did Johnnie. Lucille and Ben sat down on either side of him. Nobody said anything.

After a very long while, Uncle Eric made a big sigh, "These are definitely Masonic type rituals. The French one is a translation of the Latin one. And the other papers seem to be records of all types. I would appreciate greatly if you would lend these papers to me for further study, Ben."

"Sure. Go ahead. They probably ought to be in some Masonic archives. In fact, I've been thinking lately that maybe I'd like to get into the Masons. Maybe because I've been living in lodge rooms all my life, practically," and he started to laugh.

Uncle Eric grinned and slapped Ben on the back. "O.K. We'll get on it right away," he said.

Ben went on. "Funny thing. I don't know for sure if my father was one or not. Guess I was too young to pay too much attention. I still have boxes of his papers somewhere up in the attic and I seem to recall— Oh yes! I remember now! He had a special type of funeral, and some men put a white apron on him."

Uncle Eric shook Ben's hand and pumped it hard. "We will get on it immediately," he said quietly.

❖❖❖

Chapter 13

During Christmas holidays, Aunt Cora and I were alone because both Uncle Eric and Johnnie were in San Francisco. Eda and her grandmother went to San Francisco, too, to stay with Eda's mother in her apartment. Eda wrote a long letter about the winter there being ever so much warmer, but with lots of rain. And there was no snow. She wrote that her grandmother found some friends from Italy that she had not seen in a very long time and was so happy to be there that she was thinking of moving to San Francisco for good. She said that if her grandmother stayed and got her own apartment, then she and Stephen would keep both the house and the summer cottage. She said that she was coming back the day after Christmas, with or without her grandmother, because she wanted to get back to Stephen as soon as possible. And she said that she felt so bad about being away from Stephen on their first Christmas, but she would be back in time for New Year's and would make up for it.

Since Ben Lane was away for Christmas, too, Lucille and her mother came over for Christmas dinner. There was very much important business going on for the government out in San Francisco and that made it necessary for everybody in Uncle Eric's shipping company to be away. Even Eda wrote that the Captain was not home, which made her mother mad, but which made her grandmother glad because she did not like the Captain much.

Also, Uncle Eric was going to have some sort of an office in Newport and Stephen would be working there after New Year's. So there was a lot doing during the Christmas season, but not at our house.

I got to do quite a bit of writing on these quiet mornings and it was a good time to get it all down into my notebooks, which I was busy doing now:

> The tailor was sitting cross-legged on the table and looked up with interest at Boy. Boy stepped forward and handed him the letter. The tailor broke the seal open and recognized the name as that of the overseer of the Lane estate. He had never done any sewing for the Lanes and never thought he would have the honor. Now his mind jumped to conclusions that this boy was come to fetch him to take measurements. He became

excited as he read the short note and the full import of it did not strike him immediately. Finally, he realized that the note requested that there be made up a suit of clothes for a body servant in the Lane household.

At first, he felt insulted that so mean a job was requested of him. He did not think that the Boy picked him for the doubtful honor of making a suit of clothes. Then, he thought that he was being tried on his workmanship by this assignment and consequently must put in his most painstaking efforts into the clothes.

Of course, the clothes fitted perfectly and were of the best cloth available but the tailor was not rewarded immediately by being ordered to make clothes for the master of the house. Nevertheless, Boy brought something for him to do almost every week, so that a constant revenue, small to be sure, but satisfying, flowed to him from the Lane estates. He reconciled himself to this.

One thing that Boy got out of the experience was the habit of bathing often. Never having done so, he did not like the experience at first. He knew it was necessary for white people to bathe often, but decided that it was not necessary for black ones to do so. The tailor refused to let him try on any of the new garments until he washed himself clean. Boy ran down to the stream that ran to the village and scrubbed himself clean. He was satisfied to see the water carry off the streaks of dirt. He ran about till he was dry, put on his dirty tatters again and returned to the tailor who still wrinkled his nose in disgust.

In time the tailor developed a grudging affection for this quietly swift and efficient little black.

Of course, a similar thing happened at the bootmaker's.

Boy brought orders to make garments for his master, in time, but at the moment he had the best fitting clothes of any in the household. The tailor, still thinking that he was being tried out, did his best work on all orders.

Boy had never had such beautiful garments and did not know that the reason he did not feel constrained in them as he thought he would was because of the fit. He was prepared to feel discomfort in exchange for his magnificent appearance. He had seen Mose tug at his collar and wriggle his shoulders and heard him complain at the necessity of wearing clothes that impeded movements. Boy had not begun distinguishing the difference between clothes and quickly put down Mose as a teller of untruths.

The same with the shoes. Never having worn them, he was prepared to have his feet hurt, as he had seen some of the house servants trying to wear the cast-off shoes given to them to wear. None of the blacks had ever had shoes made to order.

Then the day arrived that Boy stepped forth and surveyed himself fully clothed in his plain but elegant finery. Grandmother Lane gave him underclothes, hose and shirts, that had been worn by her son when he was a boy and which she had put away somewhere in her domain next to the nursery. Boy's heart was pounding so joyously that he had a humming in his ears. He could hardly swallow and did not know whether to cry or laugh. He wanted to jump and shout with gladness but stood quietly in front of old Mistress Lane's French full-length mirror and kept looking at himself and disbelieving the vision. He knew that he was the only slave in the entire estate that had his clothes made for him.

The others had to pick the nearest fit from castoffs or garments bought from the usual tailor the family ordered work from, who had apprentices learning tailoring and sold the results of the apprentices' practicing.

When Quaker John gave Boy the note, he assumed that Boy would go to Mose who would first go through the pile of castoffs, and if none were found that could be worn, then he would take Boy to the tailor where the cheap ready-made garments were available. But Boy went to the Grandmother instead, and she sent him to the tailor.

When the bill arrived, the overseer-secretary paid it, thinking it was a debt incurred by the elder Lane who was always trying different craftsmen and tailors, not realizing, either that it was the fit rather than the material which makes the clothes. Thus, Lane, Senior was ignorant of the fact that the poorest-regarded tailor in the village, was the best one of them all. Quaker John was not the wiser, either. Thus, Boy became the best dressed one in the household.

Boy did not tell the grandmother everything. He always answered her questions truthfully, but did not volunteer any remarks on his own initiative.

The days after the excitement of getting settled in the nursery and getting clothed, proceeded in an uneventful procession. No longer was Boy fearful of blows and of always being hungry. He was fed and clothed, and, what is more, he belonged!

And such a belonging! The highest possible station a slave could hope to attain, was to be a personal attendant of someone in the family of the household. Now, he could come and go without other servants' questionings.

Then one day the child said, "Boy!" In the midst of cooing and gurgling he came out with the first coherent word he was heard to utter.

He never said, "Mama," or "Papa," or "Dada," as he never heard these terms. In time he came to call his grandmother, "Foufou," because of the way she had of sucking her lips against her toothless gums, which made that kind of noise.

He loved her greatly, but he loved Boy more. The grandmother was very noisy always. She started imposing tasks on him as soon as he grew a little. He was only four when she started to teach him to read. Boy learned at the same time and whispered the words to little Ben as he sat at his grandmother's knees and learned. The old woman's ears were very sharp and Boy stayed out of the reach of her thimbled finger with which she rapped his pate if he prompted, as she sat sewing and teaching Ben. She held her sewing way out in front of her, and Boy would laugh and duck out even farther out of her reach, then lean forward again to study over little Ben's shoulder.

In time they both started to learn how to write and Boy helped little Ben all the time.

Little Ben loved Boy most of all probably because his was the first face he came to recognize. That face meant security and nice pleasant noises that lulled him to sleep. The baby never had to cry to get attention. He made inquiring gurgles when he felt any discomfort and the familiar face of Boy always appeared above him.

When he was learning to walk, it was Boy who guided his steps and picked him up when he fell down.

Somehow, by some unexplained process which nobody fathomed, he emerged unspoiled. Perhaps Foufou nipped any show of selfishness in the bud.

In their own way, these three human beings were very happy. Their happiness lay in that they did not think of themselves, but of each other. And when the time came, they delved into the wisdom contained in books.

Meanwhile, Benjamin Lane, Senior, thought he would advance himself to the position of regular governor if he could get himself noticed by the governor-general of the colonies. He set out on the difficult task of making himself a favorite. The excuse of making an appointment to see the august personage had to be thought up. He remembered his newborn son and heir.

That was a sufficient excuse for creating a ball and inviting everybody. Heretofore, he had not ventured on political territory, but stayed within the society circle, and this was a very enviable circle because of its exclusiveness. Naturally, the governor-general was invited when he sent a letter that he would be present in the vicinity on government business. Lane sent his invitations out to coincide with the governor-general's visit.

And when the governor-general came, he was treated with deference and respect, but he did not belong. He felt this, of course, and fumed futilely. Such a state existed only in the colonies.

When a member of society decides to venture on a political career, he opens a breach on his side of the circle and allows the heads of a political movement to come in. The other members of society understand this lack of adherence to their strict rules, say nothing, but stand solidly behind the erring member. Soon enough, the governor-general realizes that only one member of society sends him invitations and hobnobs with him. He thinks that if he appoints the cordial one to a position of importance, the others will relax toward him. No such thing happens. With the appointment made, he still finds himself in the same position with society unless another one of the exalted decides on a political career.

When Lane thought he was being highly original with his decision to step into politics, but not bring politics into the inner society circle, he was least original because he was following a pattern set for him long before his time which will exist long after him.

Beyond a few society members who feel impelled to go into politics, there are a few who become scholars, but seldom a true leader was spawned by this ornamental class. It takes resourcefulness to become a leader and a recklessness of fortune. Few rich men want to throw away their money.

Benjamin Lane, Senior, was no different from the others in his category. But, in the scheme of things, it was imperative that he should throw himself into politics, so that he would pave the way for his son. Of course, he did this unwittingly.

Benjamin Lane, Senior, was a tall man, very lean, but a strong man. His leanness seemed to breed determination of purpose once it was aroused.

In manner, he looked like a perpetually bored man. In appearance, he was very well dressed with the latest requirement of lace and ornaments on his clothes. His hair was long and silky. He never wore a wig. Mose fixed his hair with a scented oil and tied it with velvet or silk. Well-dressed men could follow their own inclination in respect to the dressing of their hair. In effect, it was a pleasing custom.

Benjamin Lane dressed now with a touch of dignity so that he would appear soberly, worthy of position and responsibility that became a member of the governing classes.

His wife, on the other hand, blossomed out more gorgeously than ever. The best dressmakers with the latest fashion plates got her patronage. She was feverishly trying to outshine all the rest by her splendor. This extreme interest in clothes was very important, since it touched the Lane baby. Elvira has pushed the fact of her motherhood back into a recess in her brain in the first place as a very painful experience and episode. She developed an unmentioned fear that it might permanently restrict her activities. Now, she remembered that she was a mother very seldom.

The father became so absorbed in his career that he also seldom recalled his son.

Although the grandmother would have resented very much any interference by the parents in her caring for the infant, she did not forget the callous indifference on their part toward their own flesh and blood. She blamed her daughter-in-law mostly.

The Haunted House

A couple of days before Christmas Lucille dropped in on an afternoon when I was busy writing Christmas cards to send to the people who sent me one, but to whom I had not sent any.

We were having some tea and cookies when I sensed that she had something on her mind and wanted to talk to Aunt Cora without my being there, so I made up my mind to make some excuse and leave as soon as I finished my tea.

But, Lucille started right in by saying, "I am really worried about my mother. I know that she is seeing Mr. Guidice. Ever since my wedding, she has been buying her groceries in his store. Mind you, I don't object to that. I am glad that she does not have to walk clear out to the other store, specially with my not being able to carry the bags any more because Ben is very strict about it and doesn't want me to."

Aunt Cora and I were very quiet, while Lucille went on. "And then I noticed that Mr. Guidice started carrying my mother's bags home for her. And this has been going on for quite a while now."

"Well, now, Lucille," Aunt Cora murmured. "I don't see any harm in that. In fact, I think it is quite thoughtful of Mr. Guidice to carry your mother's groceries home for her."

"It has gotten to the point, Cora, that my mother no longer goes to the store any more. But Mr. Guidice brings the bags just the same—and he stays a while every time," she said ominously.

Aunt Cora spoke slowly, "Perhaps...er...she is paying him for the groceries, and...er...it takes a while to find the change."

"Well, I certainly hope so. I hope he does not have her mesmerized. And she has the weirdest things in her pantry! Things that she never bought before, Cora! All kinds of cheeses and sausages with red pepper, and even a gallon of wine under the sink that she does not know I saw."

"Now, Lucille, it is not unusual to acquire a taste for any kind of foreign cooking. In fact, a lot of it is very delicious and even better tasting than ours."

"That's exactly what my mother says. She says that Pasco—mind you, she is calling him 'Pasco' now—is teaching her to cook Italian style."

"Oh, Lucille, I think you are making more out of it than there is to it."

"Well, I don't like it, Cora. I don't like it at all."

"What don't you like about it precisely, dear?"

"To be blunt, I don't like the possibility of the idea of Mr. Guidice's being my stepfather! That's what I don't like!"

Aunt Cora thought a while and then she said, "I can remember your mother telling me on your wedding day, Lucille, how sorry she was that she had objected to your marrying Benjamin for so long and how she would give anything to make up for those empty years to you."

"Did she say that?"

Aunt Cora nodded.

"Oh, but this is different," Lucille kept shaking her head.

"Maybe it isn't as different as you think it is. Your mother was worrying what people would think of your marrying a cobbler. And it may be possible, that you are worrying what people will think about your mother marrying a grocer. Is that it?"

Just then we heard a very loud bang like a huge Fourth of July rocket going off in back of our house, and we all ran out. Then we heard a lot of people shouting from way over the back fence and we ran to the back gate into Lucille's mother's garden where the people's shouting got louder.

When we ran out the front gate, we saw first of all, Mr. Karpinski standing and yelling in Polish at the head of the steps in the middle of the block. He was waving a rifle around, and everybody was standing back. Then, he dodged inside and we ran forward to see Mr. Guidice lying face down on the snow covered sidewalk in his long winter underwear. Blood was oozing out of him onto the snow. And then some clothes came flying down and a pair of shoes from the top floor window over the front door. The last thing floating down was a grocery apron and a straw hat.

Lucille's mother who had run out onto the street first was the the only one who came to herself first and yelled for a blanket to lift Mr. Guidice onto and she ordered Lucille to call for the police and for an ambulance. I ran in with Lucille to her mother's house and we called the Rhode Island Hospital first and then the police.

Mrs. Crespi shoved everyone aside with her huge bulk and lifted Mr. Guidice onto the stretcher and got into the ambulance as it sped away, siren wailing.

The more clangorous siren of the Black Maria carried Mr. Karpinski off to jail. One of the policemen was carrying the rifle in his handkerchief covered hand and following Mr. Karpinski.

Then some street cleaners came and put sand on the blood on the sidewalk and washed everything up.

We went to Lucille's mother's house and sat in the parlor not saying anything and not looking at one another, either. Her mother had picked up all of Mr. Guidice's clothes and his shoes, apron and straw hat, and they were lying on the floor inside the front door. After a while, she got up and went over to the pile, picked everything up and went to the kitchen.

Aunt Cora motioned me to follow as she stood up to leave. She patted Lucille's hand and we left, nobody saying anything.

We waited anxiously for the paper boy to come with the Bulletin by looking out the front door practically every minute. I ran all the way to the front gate when I saw him on his bicycle. The headline was GROCER SHOT and under it in smaller letters "attempted homicide by jealous spouse". When we saw the word "attempted" we breathed with relief. The rest of the article said that it was a crime of passion by an enraged husband returning unexpectedly from work. It said that the victim was resting comfortably—on his stomach— from a grazing gunshot wound to his lower back. Aunt Cora started to laugh and laugh until the tears rolled down her face. I could not help laughing, too, at the idea of Mr. Guidice not being able to sit down for a long while.

That sure was an exciting day and I was glad that it did not end worse than it did.

❖❖❖

Chapter 14

The next portion of my Colonial times Lane's story came a couple of days after Christmas and it was a long one:

Benjamin Lane, Junior, thrived in spite of or because of parental neglect. Grandmother Lane lost no time in organizing the day into a regular pattern. What is more, the scheme was adhered to.

Sir Clinton was governor-general at the time and during his administration the first open allusions to a break with England was made. He ordered the seizure of all seditious literature and the first open hostility was announced.

Lane, Senior, hid his books more from stubbornness than patriotism. He considered himself a better man than Clinton and resented any highhandedness on the latter's part only where it concerned himself.

Clinton had been trying to get himself into society without results. And now Lane deigned to notice him. He was secretly flattered but outwardly did not display his eagerness.

Great dissatisfaction was rampant throughout the land. All the people grumbled at the taxation. However, these grumblings were not heeded. And if heeded, disregarded.

Regarding the library which Lane, Senior, hid it contained a great deal of seditious material. The sartorially minded artistocrat had a sound mind should he take the trouble to use it. He knew that the real discontent was started by the landed and wealthy ones of the land, who chafed under the greed of the ruling class of the mother country who wanted the lion's share of the wealth accumulated by the colonies. When the cry came for freedom in the following years, he knew it for what it was.

The poor and common folk were no better off after the break than before. They merely exchanged masters to pay booty to. The real benefactors of the new freedom were the wealthy ones who fattened on the labors of the workers and who paid into the new government as much as it pleased themselves to assess their wealth.

The leaders of the new government knew this but were sincerely interested in bettering conditions for everyone.

They were not at all averse to telling the right people the right thing at the right time. Some of their bluntness brightened Benjamin Franklin who was a diplomat first and citizen of the world always. The new country had only a few who were really patriots. The rest were a very good example of fence sitters. These same fence sitters were very well represented by Benjamin Lane, Senior.

On the whole, this philosophy was followed by all land and slave owners. Naturally so, because they were the ones who derived the greatest benefits from the new freedom.

The poor man became poorer, if anything. The few poor ones who realized this and lifted their voices in protest, were immediately branded as Tories. Yes, the new freedom meant heavier and securer chains for some.

The few patriots did acknowledge the necessity for the war but secretly despised and deplored the sponsors of the war who complained always that their business enterprises stood in dire peril of complete collapse.

But, all this came years later when the cry for gaining independence from the mother country gained such momentum that it could no longer be silenced without a conflagration.

At the moment, Lane, Senior, was only interested in securing for himself a position among the governing gentry of the country. Heroic men know and cope with this type of individual although oddly enough, this same element serves a purpose. Benjamin Lane, Senior, was no exception to the shallow, selfish aims of the gentry whose sole purpose of admitting an interest in the revolutionary movement was to better their wealth, as well as social standing. And, yes, he wanted to be looked up to by his peers.

Of course, when he set out on the career of a politician, the colonies were still under British rule. After the break, he merely switched his allegiance and paid the proper attention to the proper person and voiced his own opinions only occasionally. All this he did when the proper time came.

George Washington brought the highly individualistic army into line by sheer force of personality. In this way the greatest service to the new nation was rendered by him. But he was not a statesman. And his mistakes led to the clash of 1812.

Ostensibly the principal reason for the senior Lane to launch himself on a political career was to do himself justice as a man of the world and to get the envy and adulation of his fellow men. His reasons were utterly selfish. He had no notion of making the world a better place to live in for anyone else but himself.

However, the fates had set the pattern and it was his destiny to pave the way for his son whether he would or not. Then again, the wealth at his command made him useful to the new republic. What he lacked in patriotism was made up for by his son.

Through the years, many new admirers of the great and bold deeds of the founders of the new nation are vastly disillusioned when they delve into the archives of documentary matters and find evidences of selfish aims underlying the

> movements which made history. Bold actions and great daring are written up galore, but meanness abounds, also. As the movement for freedom gained momentum, it attracted all sorts of people. There were not very many who wished to take up a musket and fight.
>
> The ones who had to evade the monarchy did fight, but they were criminals, anyway. The new government got the support of pirates who now called themselves privateers and flew the stars and stripes. They went on robbing the Englishmen, who in turn had robbed the colonists of their hard earned gains. It all balanced up in the end. When all the people finally had been aroused to the need for freedom and independence, the winning of the war was assured.

All this that I wrote did not sound like my history books at all and it scared me a little. But it did sound so true to me somehow. I supposed that history books only put down the main events and could not go into just everybody's daily affairs and the reason for them.

Mr. Karpinski was still in jail under a very large bond, when Uncle Eric and Johnnie and Ben Lane came home on New Year's Eve. And Lucille came over to tell us that Ben went down to the station to bail Mr. Karpinski out. Mr. Guidice was home and refused to press charges. She also told us that the grocer blamed her mother for the whole episode, saying that it happened because she refused to marry him. And this made us all stare open-mouthed.

And what made us stare more was her telling us that her mother asked Ben to go bail "that poor man Karpinski" out. And what's more, her mother had put on the grocer's apron and was waiting on all the customers herself. Mr. Guidice still could not sit down and could only lie on his stomach in the back room on a cot, where Mrs. Grant could run in to ask questions about the stock in the store.

Eda filled me in on the rest of the story that she got from Stephen, who got it from his mother, who got it from Mrs. Crespi. It seems that widow Perrutti slammed the door at Pasco Guicide after he started paying attention to Mrs. Grant again. And Mrs. Karpinski had not been speaking to her husband for three weeks because he would not let her get some lace curtains for their parlor, so she wanted to make her husband jealous. And that's all there was to it! One did not specify how she was making her husband jealous. Anyway, Mrs. Karpinski was doing very heavy penance for three months at the church, and she had beautiful new lace curtains on her parlor windows. And everything was fine again on the lane.

Widow Perrutti was busy learning how to read, write, and speak good English from Isador Bloomstein, for nothing mind you, who lived on the first floor under her tenement, and who was a sophomore at Brown and would some day be a lawyer. He spent lots of evenings upstairs and she was now too busy to bother about the grocer.

New Year's Eve was lots of fun. Aunt Cora had a big party and Uncle Eric invited all his friends and their wives from the university and Aunt Cora had her club members come with their husbands, so our house was really packed. Lucille and Ben asked me to come with them to a party at one of Lucille's friend's house and I never in my life saw so many young guys wanting to dance with me.

I did not get to bed until the sun came up and we all had breakfast at the teacher's house. Lucille and Ben took me home and I went straight to bed.

When I woke up around noon, I got some more on the Lane story:

> When Boy had been taking care of the baby for a few months, he changed in manner, speech, and even thinking. The change was apparent to the grandmother who had no beliefs about the legality of slave ownership.
>
> However, she foresaw the terrible war to follow a long time hence that would overthrow the system.
>
> She did not tolerate familiarity with the slaves, neither did she exact cringing submissiveness. The slaves were never punished on her account. They loved her. Her influence was deeply felt although in actuality she had nothing to do with the running of the estate. She merely suggested in her irritated querulous oath-filled sentences the wisest course to follow in any event.
>
> Boy brought his problems to her. She screamed at his stupidity and waved her small fist within an inch of his unafraid nose while he listened for the inevitably wise counsel which followed the tirade. She was a good woman.
>
> The baby learned to talk at the same time it took its first toddling steps. The old woman and the little black boy held their breaths as the baby pulled himself erect by the side of a chair. The child held onto the seat and looked at them in triumph, then said, "Good!" several times.
>
> They laughed and Boy hovered around the outstretched arms to catch the baby at the first sign of his legs weakening.
>
> "Good!" they echoed the baby's pronouncement.
>
> Thus life went on for the little group apart from the ones below yet under the same roof of the two distinct households

of which Lane, Senior, was head of one; and Lane, Junior, unwittingly, was head of the other.

One day all the old slaves were herded together and taken away to the market to be sold. This was a practice commonly followed by large slave holders. A few of the old ones lucky enough to have made themselves useful around the house or had ingratiated themselves to the right persons, were kept. But, the majority were sold to slave holders not rich enough to own young and strong slaves. The old ones were sold for what could be had for them and they were worked to the limit, fed and clothed as little as possible. Rarely did these unfortunates last more than two years if that.

It was not surprising that the Lane estate resounded with laments on the day that the order was issued for all the oldsters to get ready to depart.

Grandmother Lane ordered Boy to investigate the disturbance. When he returned and told her the cause, she allowed the information to sink in slowly and make itself regarded on all sides. Perhaps, she compared herself with the old people who had outlived their usefulness. Perhaps she thought that but for the color of her skin, she, too, would have been taken off to the slave market.

For once she did not say anything beyond ordering a carriage to be brought quietly to the side entrance.

She dressed herself in her outmoded and wrinkled finery, and with the help of Boy, descended the stairs to the carriage. The news of this swept like wild fire over the slave quarter and all lamentation ceased. Boy was told to take care of little Ben and not stir from the nursery until she returned. Five of the slaves had been her own personal servants and they saw her off.

She was driven almost an hour to the city in which slaves were sold. When all the wagons had arrived bearing the old and near old slaves at the slave auction, the sales began. Usually, the traders sent notices to slave owners weeks ahead specifying date on which sale was to be held.

When Mrs. Lane arrived at the market, the slaves from her son's estate had not yet arrived. For once she was silent and sat waiting. Only her foot kept tapping the floor boards of the carriage.

As soon as the Lane slaves arrived, there began the most extraordinary sale that had ever happened. The old lady elbowed her way up to the front of the platform and bid on every old slave from her son's estate. The usually noisy square became curiously quiet as word swept through the throng that Lane's old mother was buying all the old slaves from her son. It was not lost upon them that most of them had been her own during her husband's life. Quaker John, who secretly sympathized with the old lady's actions, set out on horseback post haste to inform Lane of what was happening.

Meanwhile, Grandmother Lane bought not only her son's blacks but also all other old ones offered for sale. And it was a sale, not an auction, since no one bid against her when word spread that she was Benjamin Lane's mother. After the sale was over, the auctioneer would not take her money and tore up the tally.

The most fantastic parade wended its way back to the Lane estates. Grandmother Lane rode in the lead and the two slave-filled wagons followed. The oldsters were beside themselves with joy. Though they sang, they knew and felt afraid that the grand old lady still had her son to contend with. There were assurances among themselves that they were safe and that the old lady would be the victor, but they were not really convinced.

Following the slave-filled wagons was a group of riders, some of them owners of neighboring estates, and some who always came to auctions for diversion. And this promised to be an extraordinary diversion which would supply material for hilarious gossip for months to come in an otherwise humdrum day to day existence where nothing much happened to break the monotony. They were all eagerly anticipating Lane's and his mother's confrontation. Lane did have some detractors, many enviers, but oddly enough, no real enemies.

Before the assorted cavalcade could reach the house, the owner came galloping, followed by his informant. He pulled up sharply beside the carriage bearing his mother. She did not wait for his anger to erupt, but broke into her own, denouncing his actions, deploring his birth, and casting aspersions on his moral standards or lack of them. She even reminded him that she was the grandmother of one of the slaves on his estate, resulting from a youthful indiscretion of his. And she wound up by saying that she would buy a parcel of her own land and start her own estate. He knew that she would do it, at that.

The riders instantly formed a circle within earshot, around Lane and his mother's carriage. They were leaning forward and listening intently. Lane recognized immediately how important his next move would be. He had to emerge a hero at all costs from this situation or lose his standing in the community forevermore. At present, his political career could not stand any laughter provoking incident. Ridicule, even caused by one's own mother, would take away any dignity he might have laboriously accrued. It was no mean transition to undergo from society's fashion plate to pillar of the ruling class.

He, therefore, threw back his head and roared with laughter. He knew for a fact that none of the riders had not been guilty of like youthful indiscretions, and some of them more than once, as far as begetting issue on slave females went.

He swept off his gorgeously trimmed tricorn and slapped his horse's side until the creature reared. He went on laughing and laughing until he had to wipe his eyes with the lacy kerchief he pulled out of the cuff of his brocade coat sleeve.

When he saw that the riders also joined him in uproarious laughter and slapped each other on the back and collapsed on their horses' necks, he called out in gasping tones to Quaker John, "Hand me the money bag, sirrah! I would buy my slaves back from my mother and settle them freedmen on some corner of my lands!"

A sudden silence enveloped the encircling audience, which opened up a way for Lane, his overseer, his mother and the wagons, to proceed.

Chapter 15

It was at the end of the Spring semester around Easter and after the final tests were given, that I wrote the last segment of the story:

In fact, when Grandmother Lane made her protest against slavery in her particular fashion, she had no exalted feeling about being that single voice which preludes a movement, as in effect, she was. Her motives were consciously selfish whatever she felt subconsciously. In her mind, she was still ruler of the estate, and her son was merely taking the active part. Her daughter-in-law was nothing.

She did not go to the slave mart because of any particular affection for the blacks, but because she wanted to assert her authority. She knew she was gambling.

Meanwhile, her son was following her lead in a manner, when he conceded her victory and not because of any penitent feeling or that of altruism. His motives were selfish, too, because he did not wish to become an object of ridicule.

He swiftly devised a scheme to set the whole thing to his advantage. He freed all the old slaves and gave them five acres of his least fertile land and had a couple shacks built for them—one for the women and one for the men. Henceforth, they had to make their own living.

And, henceforth, he was known as the great humanitarian

who never sold old slaves, but gave them freedom and retired them. Whenever laughter erupted at his expense on the subject of the famous sale, he joined in and laughed the loudest. Even his detractors were impressed how he had handled the situation.

What actually happened was that the oldsters were herded into small hastily constructed shacks and left to fend for themselves as best they could. Fortunately, the remaining slaves helped the oldsters surreptitiously, even planting their vegetables and grain and starting a flock of chickens for them.

Benjamin Lane, Senior, soon put the whole episode out of his mind. He was not one to trouble himself how others felt. He thought of others only in relation to himself. In a way, his kind is admirable. When one considers them deeply, it emerges that they have an extreme lack of imagination.

Ordinarily, the episode of the old woman buying back the slaves could have made him someone to laugh at, at least for a short period. But there were too many events on the social and political scenes developing. The whole thing never got beyond mention in the immediate community. In time his custom of freeing slaves was remembered but the part played by his mother in starting the custom, was forgotten.

Benjamin Lane was too occupied with matters outside his home to bother much with matters inside. In like manner, the other members of the household were too occupied with their own affairs to bother much about what the head of the house was doing.

And when Lane became governor of the state, his family was more surprised then the neighbors, who had been watching his progress.

When Easter vacation came and Johnnie came home for a week, he read the whole story from beginning to end and marvelled a lot at it.

"When are you going to show it to the Lanes?" he asked.

"I don't know. I feel kind of silly about it, Johnnie."

"Why?"

"Oh, I don't know. It sounds like I'm a nut or something in hearing things and stuff like that."

"Well, what of it? I don't think that the Lanes will think you are a nut. On the contrary, they will think that you are something special to have this kind of gift. I think that Ben would be very interested in reading this story."

"Do you really think so?"

"I really do, Bunny, But, I think that you ought to let the Professor—," and then he laughed because he had not called Uncle Eric that for a long time. "Yeah! I think that Uncle Eric would appreciate this story more than you can imagine. He has been interested in your unusual gifts for many years. In fact, he even complained to me once, about how you always clam up whenever he wants to talk to you about it."

"O.K. I'll do it." And I stood up.

"Right now?"

"Yes."

"This I have to see."

And he followed me down the stairs into the library where Uncle Eric was sitting in his armchair near the window and Aunt Cora was sitting on his lap. We were so used to them necking all the time, that we did not notice it much any more. And Aunt Cora did not stir, only kept twisting a curl of his gray hair round and round her finger.

I put the notebooks on the desk and said, "These are the notebooks of something I have been writing for a long time. It all began when I noticed that the alley in back of our house was named Benjamin Lane. And Benjamin Lane could be the name of a man, too. So I thought about it a lot and wondered how the alley got named. And one morning as I woke up, I heard like an echo of a chime that had been struck while I was still asleep, and then I heard myself—as if I were reading to myself inwardly—a whole sentence."

Aunt Cora got off Uncle Eric's lap and they were both leaning forward and listening to me.

I went on. "Well, I told Johnnie about it and he said that I should write it down. And I did. So after that, whenever I heard the chime, I grabbed my pencil and some paper and wrote what I was hearing. And it is all in those notebooks."

Aunt Cora picked up the top one and gave it to Uncle Eric.

He opened it up and started reading out loud, "In 1756 the custom was to christen—" as I walked out of the library with Johnnie. When I looked back in the doorway, Aunt Cora had pulled up a chair and was sitting beside Uncle Eric as he continued reading.

The next morning at breakfast, Uncle Eric returned my notebooks to me before he sat down at the head of the table and stared at me. I felt very uncomfortable.

Finally, he said, "Your story is about the most fantastic thing I have ever read. When regarded as being the viewpoint of an individual, it rings true, I must say. Historically, I do not know. Are you going to show it to Ben Lane?"

"Johnnie thinks I ought to."

"I do, too. I think he will be more than interested. I know I would if I were Lane."

"O.K." I said and I picked up the notebooks.

"Right now?"

"Yes," and I made a move to get up.

"Have your breakfast first, dear," Aunt Cora put her hand on my arm. "Besides, I want to go with you when you go to the Lanes."

"Me, too," said Johnnie.

"And me, too," laughed Uncle Eric.

We made a parade as we walked through the back gate, through the Grant garden—only now it was the Guidice garden because Lucille's mother married the grocer even though he was a Catholic and had to marry her in the priest's house and not in the church—and on to the Lanes.

Lucille and Ben were surprised to see us so early in the morning, and I told them how I happened to write the notebooks. I was beginning to sound like a record to myself from repeating the same thing so many times.

Lucille was going to have a baby and she had to push herself hard to get out of the chair when she went over to look at the notebooks that I gave to Ben.

And then we all walked out again and went back home the way we came. Anyone watching us four going back and forth like that would have thought it looked pretty peculiar.

It was two days later that Lucille and Ben came to our house and Ben gave back my notebooks to me.

"I don't know what to say," he began. "But from what I have been told by my father, it seems to be true. My ancestor who built this inn was the Junior of the story. The story apparently chronicles his birth and boyhood as well as the life of his half-brother, Boy.

"I do not know the circumstances that brought him to Providence or had him become an innkeeper. Actually, the original inn that stood on this site had another name and it burned down. My ancestor rebuilt it and re-named it. I know it served as a way station for runaway slaves and served as such for three or four generations—up until the Civil War, in fact.

"Oh, yes, Eric, my father told me when I was a boy, that your house was rebuilt when a smaller one was demolished on the site. My father's father told him that. And your large house was put up to be a magnificent dwelling for its occupants."

Aunt Cora perked up her ears at that information. But Ben could not remember anything else about our house, except that it may have had some connection with the inn in some way before it was rebuilt. He also doubted if there were any public records on any of this because saving slaves and helping them run away was against the law in those days.

Chapter 16

I leaned forward to watch my friend the robin eyeing me from the swaying branch just outside my window. The window sill felt warm in the June afternoon sun as I leaned my chin on my arms and made myself more comfortable on the padded window seat.

Tonight was my high school graduation and I thought back over the past four years which seemed like forever into the future, when I was graduating from grammar school. And now it was over and it seemed like the years just whizzed by me. And yet, so much had happened.

I was glad that Johnnie had come up for my Senior Prom, even though he was the oldest guy there. I could not think of anyone else that I wanted to take to the Prom. Since Uncle Eric had opened up an office in New York City and Johnnie had transferred back east to run it, it was not as long a ride up to Providence as it had been from San Francisco.

Uncle Eric also had a small office in Newport with two people in it and Stephen was one of them. So Eda went to the Prom with Stephen and nobody knew that they were married. Lots of the Seniors remembered him from last year and they had a good time. Eda told me that she was going to have a baby, but it did not show yet, so she was safe. We were sure that if the Principal and the Dean knew that she was married and going to have a baby, she would not have been allowed to participate in the Commencement ceremonies.

Inside of me I knew that it was all right for me not to talk about it to anyone in the school. Sometimes I marvelled at what I knew to be the truth inside of me when around me everyone thought it was awful. I felt so sorry for the people back in the Middle Ages who suffered so much through such great ignorance of those who ruled over them. In some ways the same ignorance was still around.

And last night I gave a big party to all my friends in the senior class, and it was a humdinger. We played all sorts of games, and since Johnnie had come up from New York, he was at the party, too. Eda and Stephen came, of course. Ben came to help Uncle Eric and Aunt Cora chaperone the party and serve the punch and food. Lucille was expecting her baby any day so stayed home.

Anyway, the most fun I had was when we played the hide and seek game where one hides and everybody goes looking for him, or her. And when the hiding place is found, the seekers get in, too, but quietly and so that nobody will see them get in. Usually the seekers pair off. And after a long while, when the ones left cannot find the hiding place they stand and yell, "In free!" so everybody comes out. Well, I was IT and went to hide when everybody was in the library. Somebody counted to fifty and then they all came out to look for the hiding place. I purposely left the secret door under our front stairway unlatched and popped in when the count of fifty started. It was pitch black inside and I kept quiet. Pretty soon someone popped in and pulled the door shut, but must have caught a glimpse of my white dress because I heard someone groping their way toward me and I giggled and heard someone say "Sh!" very quietly. Someone must have seen the door being opened and closed because three more people got in. And then a couple more dashed in and pulled the door closed. The first person getting in got pushed against me and I knew it was Johnnie when I smelled his shaving soap. No wonder he knew where I would hide, I thought.

By this time, we were packed in pretty tight and I could feel Johnnie's heart pounding against my side. I felt like flirting a little bit with him. And, after all, he was not my real brother, he was not even related to me. So, I reached up and ran my hand over his cheek. I heard him gasp a little, then he bent his head to find my face, so I turned as much as I could when we were packed in so tight and put my arms around his neck. Oh, my! But that was a wonderful kiss! I felt it right down to my toes and felt them curl. I couldn't get enough! I wanted to go on kissing forever.

When we heard someone outside yelling, "In free!" and the door was opened by someone up front near it, it was so funny to see that most of the couples in the closet had their arms around each other and were kissing.

Well, I pretended to be shocked that I was kissing Johnnie and pretended that I didn't know it was Johnnie, and he made the same kind of motions, but his look at me from half-closed eyes let me know that he knew that I was fibbing and that I knew that he was fibbing, too.

Anyway, I did not look his way for the rest of the time and when the party broke up, I ran upstairs to my room and just lay across the bed and went over and over in my mind how Johnnie and I had kissed. And that was last night. Uncle Eric and Johnnie were out when I came downstairs this morning.

Early this afternoon, Aunt Cora had ordered me, "Now, young lady, you march upstairs and take a nap. You are still tired from last night and you must be fresh and pretty for your graduation. Scoot!" and she led me toward the foot of the stairs.

"You are going to an important ceremony tonight and we are not going to have a drooping daisy on our hands, are we?"

Of course, she was right, but sleep seemed out of the question when I had so much to think about. I looked around my room and saw the little glass ball snow-scene that Percy gave me one Christmas a long time ago, and which I kept on top of the little desk that used to belong to him. I went to my bureau and groped around under the paper which lined one of the drawers until I found the picture of Percy when he was little. I lay across the bed holding his picture in my hands and looking at it. Then I closed my eyes for a bit.

The next thing I heard was a loud knocking on my door and Uncle Eric's voice, "Bunny! Time to get up! Time to come down to dinner. Time to get ready for your graduation."

I sat up and blinked. I was still holding Percy's picture.

"All right! I'm up! I'll be down in a minute," I called back.

I sat still for a bit and recalled a most vivid dream. It was so real and it was in color. There were mountains and they were covered with purple flowers. I seemed to be standing in the middle of a road and looking through an open gate into a garden full of flowers of all kinds and colors. There was a stone house inside the garden and the house had a thatched roof on it.

As I watched, a little boy about five or six years old came out. He was all dressed up in a Scottish outfit—kilts, jacket, bonnet, everything. And the little boy was Percy. He looked like the little picture I was holding in my hands.

Then the scene changed. I found myself on the shore of a swift running river. I heard someone calling my name, and there was a tall young man on the other side. He was wearing a navy uniform with the cap set at a jaunty angle.

It was Percy.

I waved to him and called, "Come back! Come back!"

He waved, too, but the river started widening and his figure receded, but I heard his answering call, "I'm coming! I'm coming!"